THE MILL CREEK IRREGULARS
Special Detectives

The Mill Creek Irregulars

Special Detectives

by

AUGUST DERLETH

DUELL, SLOAN AND PEARCE
New York

for Sim and Pete
in memory of the old days in the harness shop,
along the river and in the country around
Sac Prairie . . .

Contents

THE MILL CREEK IRREGULARS

Special Detectives

1.

An Invitation to the Country

FROM where I sat in the summer-kitchen that August morning, I could hear the telephone ring. It rang loud and steadily, like a long-distance call. I unfolded a funny-paper and began to read *The Bungle Family*.

Mother called from the back porch. "Stephen! Stephen Grendon! Telephone!"

I pushed the papers aside and ran out of the building and up the back porch steps. Mother's good-looking face didn't tell me a thing, but as I went past she said, "It's Uncle Joe Stoll."

"Hello," I said into the telephone.

"Old Timer," said Great-uncle Joe in a booming voice, "I'm comin' into town this afternoon an' fixin' to bring you along out. You ain't been out for so long we're kinda for-gittin' what you look like."

"Gosh, Uncle, I'd like to come," I said, "but . . ."

"I'll talk to your Ma," he hollered. Great-uncle Joe always shouted into the telephone. He thought that the farther away you were, the louder he had to talk.

"It's not Ma," I said. "It's Sim Jones—I promised him we'd go fishing this afternoon."

"Fetch him along. A couple-a weeks in the country'll do him good. He's mighty skinny. You can go fishin' in the millpond. Now go ask your Ma."

"I'll have to ask him, too," I said. "Take your time coming in."

Out in the kitchen, Mother laughed. "Uncle Joe always takes his time—as if you didn't know."

I said good-bye to Great-uncle Joe and went into the kitchen.

"Well?" asked Mother, her full eyebrows raised and her blue eyes twinkling.

"Ma, they want me to come out. Sim Jones, too."

"I don't know, Stephen. In two weeks or so school begins. It's time you looked into your books."

"Oh, Ma," I said, "you know I always do my studying in school. I never bring my books home."

Just then the porch screen door slammed, and Grandfather Adams came in. He had his hat pushed back on his head, and was shoving his lower lip up against his moustache, as if he had been chewing something. His sharp eyes went from Mother to me.

"What's up now?" he asked, pulling a chair out from the table with one foot and sitting down on it. "Seems like every time I set foot in this house you two are at it."

"Pa, my children must learn to obey me," said Mother firmly.

"What's he done now?" asked Grandfather Adams, his eyes laughing.

"Just as if I'm always doing something!" I cried. "It's

only that I want to go out to Great-uncle Joe's, and Ma thinks I better stay home and start to study for school. It's still vacation time."

"I didn't say you couldn't go," said Mother. "Some day that chip on your shoulder'll fracture your collar bone."

Grandfather Adams grinned. "Always let a woman talk herself out first, before you argue with her," he said. "Mothers are no different from other women."

"Pa!" cried Mother. "You fill his head with all kinds of ideas."

"Ideas make the world go round, Rose," said Grandfather.

"May I go, then?" I asked. "Because I have to go down and try to talk Sim into it, and he'll think of every objection he can raise."

Mother threw up her hands. "Oh, go! Go! I'll never hear the end of it if I don't give in."

I grinned at Grandfather and got out fast, before Mother changed her mind. I could hear her talking as I went down the porch steps. "Now, Pa," she was saying, "it's time we had an understanding about that boy." That was Mother all over; she was always after "understandings" just as if she didn't know there wasn't much you could pin down and keep pinned down that way because everything you did depended on different circumstances the "understandings" didn't cover.

I ran across the lawn and the field to the railroad tracks. I had to wait there while the train went past. Harry Jefferies was driving the locomotive, and I waved to him.

He leaned out and hollered, "Hello, there, Steve. You all set to grow up and be an engineer?"

"Sure," I said. "I'll be driving her any day now."

He just laughed. I wished I had time to show him. I wished I knew *how* to show him. Maybe some day when I had done all the things I figured on doing when I got older, I'd get around to learning how to drive a locomotive, too. Then I'd climb up into the cab and invite old Harry to sit down and away I'd go out of Sac Prairie to Mazomanie so fast it'd make old Harry's hair white by the time we came within sight of Mazomanie. . . .

The train was past. I crossed the two sidings and the main line, and went into the Freethinkers' Park, where the well-worn path led from the northwest corner to the southeast. I ran along the path and down to the street-corner on the other side of the big old Park Hall, where the Freethinkers held their meetings. Then down the street and in along Sim Jones' house.

Sim's mother was just coming out on to their little screened-in back porch. She was a short, trim woman, small-boned, with gravely thoughtful eyes that were quick in their movements, like a bird's.

"Ach, Stephen!" she said. "How's Mama?"

"Fine," I said. "Is Sim here?"

She shook her head. "He went down to the shop quite a while ago."

"Thanks," I said, and started away.

"If you see him," she called after me, "tell him he forgot his rubbers. I see some clouds in the southwest. It might rain."

"Sure," I said, "I'll tell him."

I ran down the alley, across Dresen's corner, to the back walk which led into the harness shop, a two-storey building, which pushed back on its narrow lot and made a cozy corner at the back door. In Spring lilies-of-the-valley and a spreading flowering wild currant and a snow-apple tree made the whole yard smell for weeks like the woods along the brook where all the wild flowers grew.

Old Fred Jones was standing at the secretary when I came in. He had had the door above the slanted writing desk open, but he closed it in a hurry when he heard me. He had just taken a nip from a bottle of whisky he kept there, but Sim and I never let on we knew about it. Old Fred was a broad-shouldered man, with a poorly-kept moustache, and blue eyes that sometimes looked through his spectacles at you, but most of the time appeared to look over or around them. He seemed mild and innocent, but he was a lot more clever than he looked.

"Well, well," he said cheerfully, "the lost Charley Ross! Where you been all this time?"

"They sold me into slavery," I said. "Me and Dorothy Arnold. Is Sim here?"

Old Fred smiled a little, bent his head back, and looked up toward the ceiling, where all the racket was going on. "The boy's putting John's room to rights for him," he said.

Up over the harness shop there were rooms for rent, and one had been rented that summer to John Ganzer. John was a fat old man whose legs were giving out on him. He wheezed terribly when he went up or down the stairs. "Arthur-itis," he said he had in his legs. He sometimes came downstairs to sit and talk with us. He told the tallest stories we ever heard—all about his adventures. We used to look at him and listen without cracking a smile until he ended up with, "I guess you poys don't believe me." He always said "poys," never "boys." He kept a car out in back, and sometimes he drove off in it, all over town, always in second. High was too fast for him. But he told all his stories in high, and after he lurched out of the shop we got sore sides laughing.

"Should I go up?" I asked.

"John's up there," answered Fred. "If you go up, you'll never get a word in edgewise. Better wait. Sim'll be down any minute."

Fred crossed the shop to the long work-bench running the length of the north wall up past the middle of the shop toward the front. He sat down on the stitching-horse, pulled over his little tin, and emptied some Asthmador into it. He lit the green powder and sat with his head wreathed in the smoke rising up from it. He had asthma, and he had to sniff up the smoke several times a day.

I went over to the step-ladder near the secretary along the south wall and sat down there. It was cool in the shop, as always. Maybe it was because there were no windows on the south, and some storage room separated the building from the hot sun on that side. Maybe having both doors open helped, so the air could move through from the west or the east. The Wisconsin River ran past just on the other side of Main Street in front, and its freshness came in morning and evening.

Fred finished inhaling the Asthmador and walked to the back door to empty the ashes from the tin.

"It's hot," he said, when he came back.

"Sure is," I agreed. "I ran all the way down. I sure can feel it."

"So far, 1922's hotter than the summer of 1921 was," said Fred reflectively. "Nothing like it was in the old days, though. I remember when I was in the Philippines—oh, my, a body just sweat all the time!"

Fred Jones was a veteran of the Spanish-American War. He never talked about it much, though. He sat down on the stitching-horse once more and put two pieces of leather in the clamp so that he could sew them together. He had a monster callus on his right thumb from all the sewing he did—pulling the needle through that tough leather.

The noise stopped upstairs. I could hear Sim coming down. Fred timed him, and just as Sim stepped into the shop from the side door around the corner from the back door, he said, "Look what the wind blew in!"

"It was this afternoon we were going fishing—not now," said Sim, before I had a chance to say a word.

His lean face was flushed a little, as if he had been working too hard. More likely he was just annoyed, because he hadn't planned on me before afternoon, and he didn't like his plans altered.

"Plan's changed," I said. "I'm going out into the country this afternoon—to Stolls. Great-uncle Joe said to invite you along. We'll be out there ten, twelve days or so. Maybe two weeks. You game?"

Sim looked at me as if I had just asked him to take a quick trip to the moon. "Can't fish in the country," he said.

"You forget the millpond's in walking distance. And the Ferry Bluff down along the river's not much farther."

"You can fish for more than fish," said Old Fred without turning around. "The more a man fishes for in this life, the more he's apt to find out."

"Besides," I went on, "you can never tell what might turn up out there."

"Ja, work," said Sim bitterly. "I used to go down to McGregor on the train with Ma to see my uncle. He lived on a farm, too. Plenty of work all the time."

"You got all the qualifications," I said. "I heard you just now. I'll bet John's room looks like new."

Sim grinned.

"Anyway, you know Great-uncle Joe and work are sworn enemies," I went on. "And now Gus Elker's Justice of the Peace and Ed Burke's got deerhounds and any time you get homesick you can go down to the Fair Valley Store or the Mill Store and hear as much oil poured as you ever hear in the harness shop."

Old Fred chuckled. "Neatsfoot is the best," he said. "Jones' Harness Shop carries only the best."

"And Pa only pours the number one best," added Sim, "except when he's tired." Whenever Old Fred made casual small talk, Sim called it "pouring oil."

"What about it?" I said to Sim.

"We'll see."

"Oh, that's what you always say," I said. " 'We'll see!' What you mean is you want to wait around and see if anything better turns up. Besides, Great-uncle Joe's coming this afternoon to pick us up."

"Don't rush me," said Sim nervously. "This afternoon! Not everybody can change his mind as fast as you can. You and I had it all arranged to go fishing this afternoon."

"I said we'd go," I answered. "We'll go fishing in the millpond. I know every hole there. I always go out with Grandpa Grendon or Grandpa Adams. Listen, I can take you to a place that's so thick with sunfish and bluegills you can hardly see the water."

Old Fred turned around and looked at me. "You been listening to John Ganzer?" he asked.

"Well, it's *almost* that full of fish," I said.

"What's there to do in the country?" asked Sim.

"The country is the best place in the world to grow up," put in Old Fred. "You town boys think you have to go to a movie every other night, or watch a parade, or go in and out of the stores. You think you can't do without the medicine shows and Brooks' Stock Company and Buster Brown coming to town to sell shoes. Get out once where the birds sing and the other animals are. . . ."

"Other animals?" I hollered.

"Sure. What makes you think you ain't an animal, too?"

I had never thought about it. It was certainly a different idea.

Old Fred smiled. He looked up out of the window over the north wall bench as if he were looking into the next county. "A man who grows up next to fields and woods— he never forgets it. It's something in his blood—it's the best thing he can have to carry along with him when he gets old. . . ." Then he half closed his eyes and was still.

"Well, what about it?" I asked Sim.

"I don't think Ma'd like it."

"That reminds me—when I went past your place, she said to tell you you forgot your rubbers."

Sim sighed. "You see how it is? If I go out into the country, I'll have to take rubbers and my umbrella and my raincoat. That's just the beginning. Then all the medicines she thinks of. Oh, you don't know what it's like!"

I didn't say anything. I sympathized with Sim. I also sympathized with Mrs. Jones. I knew Sim had had a little brother once, and the boy had died; now Sim was all Mrs. Jones had, and that was why she always worried so. But Mrs. Jones didn't seem to realize that Sim was the soul of caution. There was nobody more practical than Sim. He didn't take anything for granted. He had to have the proof of it—something he could see or touch. Just reasoning wasn't enough for Sim.

"How're you going to know whether you'd like the country unless you try it once?" I asked. "You don't take my word for it. Nor your Pa's."

Old Fred cleared his throat. That was a sign he was getting tired of all this useless talk. "Go," he said to Sim. "Do you good. I can get along without you for a couple-a weeks."

"You mean go to the farm?" asked Sim as if he couldn't believe it.

"Sure, sure. The work can wait, now you got John taken care of. But you better go home and ask Mother."

"I know Ma," said Sim, as we went out the back door. "She'll raise heck if I'm away from home that long."

"Hoh! Great-uncle's farm is only six-seven miles out of Sac Prairie. If you get homesick, you can get back into town easy. You could even walk it. Somebody's always driving in, though."

Sim didn't answer. I could tell by the look in his eyes that he was thinking it all over. I watched his face as much as I could walking beside him. I figured part of him wanted to go and part didn't; I figured he was counting on his mother to say no, he couldn't go.

Mrs. Jones was in the kitchen, cutting beans. The kitchen in the Jones house was the only room that was really lived in. All the rest were filled up with whatnots and fine horsehair furniture made of black walnut and mahogany, and beautiful pictures and rugs, and they were so spotless they looked as if nobody ever stepped into them.

I explained everything to Mrs. Jones, while Sim stood there with a kind of smirk, as if he knew what to expect.

Then Mrs. Jones smiled and said, "Sure, Sim can go. As long as you're along, Stephen, he surely can go."

Sim looked goggle-eyed.

"I often wish Sim could be more like you, Stephen," she added.

Sim gave me a hard look. If looks could kill, I'd have been stone cold that second. I knew just how he felt. Once, when Carlie Ganzlin was up playing at my house, something like this had happened to me. Carlie was a little devil, but whenever he came to my place he acted like an angel. And that day Grandmother Adams had scolded me and said, "Why can't you be a good little boy like Carlie?" And Carlie took it, smirking and grinning. I got so riled up I just grabbed a broom and hit him over the head. Right about now, I could just feel that broom.

Sim looked resigned. "All right," he said. "I'll try it. But I'm not saying I won't be home tomorrow."

"We'll pick you up here as soon as Great-uncle comes," I said. Then I got out before he could change his mind.

2.

Trouble at Riley's

GREAT-UNCLE JOE was late, all right.

It was past four o'clock when Grandfather Adams came into the house by the back door and said, "Looks like Joe coming. There's enough dust clouding up behind him to shut out everything he's passed."

"Is he driving the car?" asked Mother apprehensively.

"He is. Should have brought the surrey. The horses have the sense Joe loses when he gets behind that wheel."

"Now, Pa!"

"Well, Rose, it's true. Your mother's brother can be counted on to do any crazy thing he gets into his head. Makes things lively, though, boy," he added to me.

Great-uncle Joe's Model T drew up outside in a mass of billowing dust, out of which he stepped like a genie. He had on a straw boater and a linen duster, but underneath the duster he wore his regular farm overalls. Great-uncle was a heavy-set man, with a thick, jowled face, and in that outfit he was a sight to see.

He swept into the house through the front, shouting, "Hello, Rosie! Hello, Adams!—They ain't caught up with

14

you yet, hah?—Come on, Old Timer—we ain't got all day."

"The only reason you haven't is that you've used most of it up," said Grandfather Adams.

"Never see a man like you, Adams," said Great-uncle Joe. "Always wantin' to start arguments."

Grandfather fixed his eyes on Great-uncle's duster. "Where on earth did you find that, Joe?"

"Out at my place. I went into the corncrib—that big one over 't t'other end a the barn, and there it hung. I recollec' I won it in a raffle at the Old Settlers' Picnic ten years ago, maybe more, and I figure I might's well git some of the wear out of it."

His guileless blue eyes twinkled. His red cheeks shone. He brushed at his thick moustache and looked proudly all around at us.

"Nobody shot at you down town?" asked Grandfather.

"Hoh!" snorted Great-uncle.

"It goes to show how the human race is softening," observed Grandfather.

"I don't know how you can stay so sweet, Rosie," said Great-uncle, "with a cantankerous old crab like that for a Pa." Then, gazing at me with concern, he said again, "Old Timer, git your things together. My old woman's like to have conniptions—I was to be back by three."

Grandfather Adams grinned. "They should have taught you how to tell time when you were still young enough to read," he said.

"I'm all packed," I said. "I've been ready since noon."

"Well, come on then," said Great-uncle, turning. Over

his shoulder he said to Grandfather, "Give my love to Lizzie."

"I think she'd appreciate a dressed chicken more," said Grandfather.

"Always thinkin' of his stomach," said Great-uncle. "I can see where you git it from, Old Timer. Is that Jones boy comin' along?"

"Yes," I said. "We have to go round and pick him up."

Mother followed us to the door. "Behave now, Stephen. Do what Aunt Lou says. And you send him right home if he doesn't, Uncle," she said.

"Why, Rosie, he's as good as gold," said Great-uncle Joe.

"I want to live to see that day," said Mother fervently.

Grandfather Adams waved good-bye behind Mother.

I climbed into the front seat of the Model T, to sit up beside Great-uncle Joe. He got her started and climbed in. Oh, that car shook and choked and sputtered! It drowned out the grain elevator down at the end of the block. Great-uncle said something, but I couldn't hear what it was. Mother was shouting something, too. I just nodded; that seemed to satisfy her.

We started. The Model T jumped away from the side of the road like a cat. Up to the corner, around it on two wheels, and down around the block past the park to Sim's place. It was a lucky thing she threw up so much dust Mother couldn't have seen how we took that first corner.

Sim was waiting. He had been waiting since noon. His face was as dark as a thunderhead. He was a stickler for time. If he said noon, he meant noon. To come past four o'clock was just about equal to committing a capital crime.

He marched out with his things. He had them setting

on the front porch—two bags, his fishing paraphernalia, even his stamp collection. He hardly even saw Great-uncle Joe for the look he gave me.

"I thought you said right after noon," he said to me.

"I did. Only Great-uncle Joe was held up."

"Git in, boy," said Great-uncle in a hearty voice at the same time he tipped his hat to Mrs. Jones, who had come to the door, hearing the car's commotion. "We'll take good care of him, Mrs. Jones," he bawled.

"I wasted all that time," said Sim.

"Time," hollered Great-uncle Joe. "What's time?"

"Time is the most valuable thing I own," said Sim.

"You don't own it," said Great-uncle flatly. "You only spend it."

He waved once more to Mrs. Jones, and we roared off down the street. Great-uncle Joe headed right for the river road, past the old livery stable, past the biggest brewery in town, past the railroad bridge, and turned west on the Lower Mill Road.

The Model T bumped along raising all the dust there was to be raised. Sim began coughing, and I had to cough some, too. Great-uncle just sat there like a king behind the wheel; he never seemed to notice a thing. He was proud of his car, he was proud of his driving, and the way he drove he figured everybody's eyes were on him. It was a cinch nobody missed us going by. The Lower Mill Road was an almost straight stretch west of town to where it met Highway 60, and Great-uncle Joe certainly let that old Model T out. We must have been going all of fifty! Even the cows we passed looked up when we went by.

Oh, but that was a ride! We got bounced and banged around. The baggage was jumping, too. Once, when I looked back at Sim, I saw him bumping up and down like the bags. He was as white as a sheet and hanging on for dear life, with his teeth gritted and his face grim, and determined to come out of it all alive.

Great-uncle didn't seem to mind. In fact, he was so well pleased with the good time we were making that he hummed now and then and sang a few snatches of songs. *In the Good Old Summer Time* and *Red Wing* and *Pony Boy*. And once in a while he bellowed at me.

"The Ford," he hollered, "is a wonderful invention!"

He didn't expect any answer.

A little later, he said, "The Ford is a revolution all by itself!"

Once, when he got a good look at me, he leaned over and shouted, "You feelin' all right, Old Timer?"

The car almost left the road that time, but he got her righted.

When we reached Highway 60, we had to go slower. For one thing, there was more traffic, since the junction was right at the old Mill Store near Grell's millpond. For another, the road from there on was full of curves. So Great-uncle had to slow down, and Sim and I breathed again.

And now, with the lessening of the dust, we could see the country. The creek, blue under the hot August sun, and the groves of old maples and elms along the road and beside the sloughs near the falls that poured out of the millpond just above the bridge we crossed when we went over the creek. Grell's mill stood up along the pond on our right, and Grell's house was lost in trees between the mill and the road.

The highway wound around the south side of the Mill Bluff and the hills beyond, past the Fair Valley Store, and then up into the hills, where Great-uncle Joe Stoll's farm lay in a gentle valley just south of Gus Elker's and Stone's Pocket, and west of Ed Burke's place, which lay between Great-uncle's farm and the grand Ortell house on the top of the Mill Bluff.

Great-uncle Joe scattered chickens right and left when he drove into the farmyard. They flew squawking in all directions and brought Great-aunt Lou to the back porch.

Great-aunt Lou was a small woman, compared to Great-uncle Joe. She was medium in height for a woman, on the thin side, even though her full skirts and the apron she almost always wore made her look bigger than she was, and just about the kindest person I knew outside of home. Right now, though, she was looking over her spectacles out of narrowed eyes at Great-uncle Joe, and her mouth was pursed up as if it had been holding in a lot of things she was waiting to say.

The car sputtered and died.

"You're right on time," she called out, "—for supper."

"Now, Lou," said Great-uncle placatingly.

"Five o'clock! My conscience!"

"Mine, too," muttered Sim, under his breath.

Sim was looking around to take his bearings. He had got down out of the Model T and was still hanging on to the car. He was a little shaky. Sim had been out to the farm just once before; that was mostly at night, when we were on our way down the Wisconsin on a raft earlier that summer.

Great-aunt Lou never stopped to hear what Great-uncle had to say. She was giving him a piece of her mind, a good-sized piece.

"I might of known it'd turn out like this," grumbled Sim. "I ought to have my head examined for listening to you."

"Wait," I said. "We just got here."

"That's the trouble," said Sim. "First I sit around waiting till past four o'clock. Then I get all shook up in this vehicle. Now it don't look as if we'd go fishing at all today."

"The sun won't set for hours," I said, "and they bite in the millpond more so in the evening than in the heat of the day."

Great-aunt Lou finished with Great-uncle Joe and turned to us. "You poor boys!" she said. "You must be half starved. It's a lucky thing I got supper ready. Heavens t' Betsy! That man of mine never thinks on a soul but himself. You come right in and set to table."

Sim brightened considerably. The thought of food revived him the way a drooping violet perks up when you put it into water.

"Just bring your things in. Take them right up to the attic. You know where 'tis," she said.

I led the way into the house, up the stairs, and into the attic room, which was a pleasant place, with dormer windows and gable windows and the roof low overhead, making everything cozy. There was enough circulation to keep the place cool, and a big elm shaded it outside.

Sim had shot a good look at the table when we went through the kitchen. It was loaded, the way it always was.

"Roast chicken!" murmured Sim, licking his lips. His eyes gleamed. "And cherry pie!"

"Oh, they'll fatten you up out here, Sim," I said. "Nobody cooks any better'n Great-aunt Lou!"

"Well, let's get at it," said Sim.

We clattered down the stairs.

Great-uncle Joe and Great-aunt Lou and the hired man—a fellow of about thirty-five named Burl Wilkins, who never said much to anybody—were already sitting at the table, waiting for us. As soon as we sat down, Great-aunt Lou said grace, and we pitched in.

"It sure does a body good to see somebody eat," said Great-aunt.

She said this just about every time I ate there. It always made me feel guilty. "Sim's the one who can eat," I said.

"He needs to," said Great-aunt, examining him critically. "The poor boy looks underfed."

"Nothing puts any meat on me," said Sim. "I could eat a horse."

"Me—it all goes to muscle," I said.

"Well, that ain't what my old woman calls it when it's on me," said Great-uncle Joe with a loud guffaw.

"Joe," said Great-aunt, "Gus Elker was over twice this afternoon looking for you. Something's eatin' him."

"Oh, something always is," said Great-uncle casually.

"'Peared to me it was serious," said Great-aunt Lou.

"Hoh! How can a body tell?" Great-uncle wanted to know. "Gus's face always looks as if he jest lost his lead coon dog. Anyway, he'll be back. Right now, all I feel like is eatin'."

We had finished supper, and the hired man had gone out to do chores, when Gus Elker came. We had moved out to the back porch to enjoy the cool of evening, and Gus came down the lane around the barn. He was a short man—not exactly what you'd call "little"—and he always wore overalls a couple sizes too large for him and an old felt hat with holes in it through which his strawy hair stuck out. He had a kind of moon-like face—round, with a straggly yellow moustache curved in a crescent above his mouth. His eyes were what you remembered—they looked like the eyes of a dog that has just been punished, soft, reproachful, and they gave his whole face a sad look.

"Hello, all," he said, as he came up.

"Set a spell, Gus," invited Great-aunt Lou.

"Thanks, Ma'am, Mrs. Stoll, I reckon I will."

He sat down on the edge of the porch and gazed off with a troubled air into the northwest, past the farmyard to the woods, where the westering sunlight still lay pinkly on the treetops. Great-uncle waited for him to say something; he looked toward him expectantly once or twice, while Great-aunt Lou sat there with a little smile on her face, like somebody waiting for the show to begin.

"Well, what's eatin' off'n you?" asked Great-uncle at last.

"Joe, I don't rightly know, but I figger I'm in a fix," said Gus with a deep sigh.

"What you done now?"

"Me? I ain't done nothin'," said Gus, aggrieved.

"Be careful, Gus," warned Great-aunt Lou. "That man of mine's just as like as not to make your fix worse as to unfix you."

Gus smiled weakly and looked at her as much as to say he knew it was so, but to whom else could he turn?

"Go on, go on," said Great-uncle impatiently. "I don't aim to set here all night."

Gus sighed again. "I don't know," he said, "the books don't tell me—now I'm Justice a the Peace—do I have to wait till something happens or have I got the right to prevent it?"

"You got a fine point there, Gus," admitted Great-uncle thoughtfully. His eyes twinkled. "I be dog, if I was the Justice, if I'd go lookin' for trouble."

"I ain't never looked for trouble all my life," protested Gus vigorously. "The most I ever found I was with you, and you might say you found it, not me."

"What you're aimin' to find out is whether you have to wait till the horse is stole before you can close the door—or can you close the barn door before they steal the horse?"

"That's about it," agreed Gus.

"Gettin' something outa you is like pullin' teeth!"

"It's my bounden duty to respec' the law," protested Gus. "I sworn to uphold the law an' to administer it. I don't rightly know where I begin, that's all."

Sim caught my eye and grinned.

"Besides," Gus went on, as if he had seen Sim, "I don't aim to be the laughin' stock a Sac Prairie."

"Hoh!" snorted Great-uncle. "People'll laugh at a body if they're minded to—they don't need no reason, not but what, when they see you in those overalls too big for you, they ain't got reason."

"I need the circulation," said Gus. "I like my clothes roomy. I like to die if I had to walk around all pushed together tight like you do, you old pot-belly!"

"Well, what does the law-book say?" asked Great-uncle.

"Says it's my duty to administer the law in my distric' as long as it's in my jurisdiction. An' it sure is—right under my nose, you might say." He paused. "Only, it ain't been brought up before my court yet," he added.

"Well, then, what is it?" pressed Great-uncle.

"Trouble is, I don't rightly know."

Great-uncle's exasperation boiled over. "You got it in your head something's up somewheres, but you don't rightly know," he said. "What kind of a notion is that, anyway? I been thinkin' a long time you been gettin' a little weak in the head, Gus. Now, out with it!"

Gus sort of pulled himself together and said, almost apologetically, "I got a feelin' something's goin' on at Jake Riley's. He keeps to the house like a old crow. Ain't workin' his fields. Ain't doin' anything. Jest settin' there. Ain't friendly. Ain't wantin' to come out to talk."

"Hoh! Jake Riley's jus' fat and lazy," said Great-uncle. "He ain't never been too friendly."

"An' I ain't seen hide nor hair a his stepdaughter," finished Gus.

Great-uncle Joe was gathering himself for another withering attack when Great-aunt laid a restraining hand on his arm.

"Come to think of it," she said quietly, "I ain't seen Molly for quite a spell."

Gus grasped at this straw. "That's it, Ma'am—that's jest it!"

"And that ain't natural," concluded Great-aunt Lou, casting the die in Gus Elker's favor.

3.

We Decide to Investigate

For a full minute, nobody said anything. The sunlight was drawing away now, and the first thin dusk was creeping in from the east. In the silence, the farmyard sounds rose clearly—chickens cackling, pigs grunting, cows moving in the barn, one of Great-uncle's dogs barking down in the Pocket, pigeons cooing on the barn roof.

"Not that I seen anything," said Gus then. "It's jest that I didn't see what I ought to've seen."

"Now, Gus, you tell it your way," said Great-aunt Lou persuasively. "I declare to goodness, that man of mine can't keep hisself from putting in his two cents' worth. You, Joe, you listen."

Encouraged, Gus began to talk. He had gone over to Jake Riley's place, which was north of his farm, over in the Skunk Hollow almost near the Witwen road, to ask Molly to come over and give his housekeeper a hand canning beans. Jake had met him at the back door, denying him entrance, saying Molly didn't feel well and was lying down.

"Maybe she was," put in Great-uncle.

"Sure, maybe so," agreed Gus. "But why'd he ac' so funny? Lettin' me stan' outside? He never done it before."

Gus went on. He told how he had come past Jake Riley's place two days later. He had seen someone watching him from the window. It had not looked like Jake. The way Gus made out, it was Molly, and she had seemed frightened. So he had turned in. Once again Jake had met him at the door. This time, in reply to a question about Molly, he had said she was off visiting somewhere. But the curtain at the window still waved a little, as if somebody had stepped away from it, when Gus left—and Jake was still in the doorway.

"An' there ain't nobody else but them two on that farm," said Gus. "I kep' a eye on Jake's place after that. Time an' again I seen him on the porch—turnin' to talk to someone inside—but I never seen Molly set foot outside that door, an' I seen somebody in her room. So I put two an' two together, an' I figger Jake's got her locked up in the house."

"Ever' time you put two and two together, Gus, you git five or six—any number but four," said Great-uncle scornfully. "Like as not Molly needed punishin' and got sent to her room."

"Molly's a good girl," said Great-aunt Lou tartly.

"And then, this mornin', that feller came," finished Gus.

"What feller?" asked Great-uncle.

"I don't know who he was. A stranger to me. He asked all about Jake."

"What did he ask, Gus?" put in Great-aunt.

"Oh, lots a things," said Gus airily, waving one hand. "Wanted to know if Jake worked his farm. If he hired any new men lately. If he lived alone. If he went out much. If he did—where did he go? Don't make no sense to me, but he seemed a real smart young feller."

"Somebody from hereabouts?" asked Great-uncle, frowning.

"I tol' you—a stranger," said Gus. "Foxy, too. Dressed up like a hunter. I says to him, 'You huntin'? I'm the Justice a the Peace,' I says, 'an' the season ain't open.' 'Foxes,' he said. 'No law against that, is they?' Well, there ain't, but that gun wasn't fired, I could tell it because there wasn't any powder smell."

"You're a regular Sherlock Holmes, Gus," I said.

He looked at me darkly. "Who's he?"

I explained that he was the greatest detective who ever lived.

"This feller come in a car or afoot?" asked Great-uncle.
"Afoot."

"I allow that's mighty suspicious. He musta had a car somewheres."

The highway was quite a distance from Gus Elker's farm. The way the farms lay in the Pocket and on the hills around, Gus's lay beyond Great-uncle's to the north. Old man Stone's place was west and north, and Jake Riley's was on the far side of Gus's, northeast, just off the Skunk Hollow road, up in a little valley, sort of out of the way. If somebody parked a car on the highway, he'd have to walk two miles or so. If he parked on the Skunk Hollow road, he'd attract too much attention. So if a stranger was walking all the way to Gus Elker's place, hunting fox, the way he said, when he wouldn't have any reason to be hunting fox closer to the road, it would make any farmer in Gus Elker's position suspicious.

"Still and all," said Great-aunt Lou quietly, "don't seem to me it hangs together." She sat looking at Gus through the gathering dusk, her mouth pursed, her eyes slitted behind her spectacles.

"Look at this thing more reasonable-like," said Great-uncle Joe. "We all know how mean and lazy Jake Riley is."

"An' he's got plenty money," said Gus.

"No," corrected Great-aunt Lou. "It's not *his* money—he can't touch it. It was his wife's, and it'll come to Molly when she's eighteen."

"Well, he's gittin' along," said Great-uncle testily. "What I'm aimin' to say is Gus's lookin' for something to make him suspicious. Ten to one, there's some explanation. Most always is, if you look hard enough."

"You ready to go over an' find out?" asked Gus sharply.

Great-uncle shook his head. "Ain't none a my business."

"I think Gus is right," said Great-aunt Lou. "Something's going on, and I think we ought to find out what it is. My land! That poor girl's all alone with her stepfather. There's no telling what could happen—with her comin' into her money next birthday."

"He can't claim it," said Gus. "If anything happens to her, it'll go to somebody else—not Jake."

Great-uncle looked at me, grinning. "You see how it is, Old Timer. That's jest like a woman—every time. Can't abide not knowin' what's goin' on! You keep clear of 'em if you know what's good for you."

" 'Pears to me," said Great-aunt, ignoring him, "somebody ought to keep a kind of watch on Jake's place for a few days."

"Not me," said Great-uncle hastily.

"Nor me, either," added Gus. "Ma'am, he knows all of us too well."

Great-aunt Lou turned to Sim and me. "He don't know these boys. Could be he's seen Steve once or twice, but he'd never remember him."

"Hoh!" burst out Great-uncle. "Jake's place is in that pocket, and a body couldn't git close enough to look without bein' spied out. If he's up to something, he'll keep his eyes open. Jake's no fool."

"There's woods up around the south an' west of his place. On the hills," put in Gus. "A body could hide in them woods."

"That's a good piece off from the house. What'd you expect to see from there?" jeered Great-uncle.

"I know just the thing," I said. "Grandpa Adams' telescope. He used to watch the stars through it. You could put it in the crotch of a tree and keep it turned on Jake Riley's house and see just as well as if you were right there in the yard."

"Only," said Great-uncle, "we ain't got it."

"We could get it," I said. "We could call him up."

That was the moment for deciding. I looked to Great-uncle Joe; he just sat gazing thoughtfully at me, his lips pushing his moustache up against his nose, one finger stroking his ear. I looked to Gus Elker; he sat anxiously on the edge of the porch, ready to get up and run if anybody as much as said Boo! in a loud voice. I looked to Great-aunt Lou.

"Go in and call him up," she said.

I went into the house and rang through to Sac Prairie. Mother answered.

"Ma," I said, "is Grandpa there?"

"Not just now," she said. "What's the matter? Is anything wrong? Do you know you forgot your rubbers and raincoat? I told you to take them. You forgot your geometry book, too, and you know how hard mathematics comes to you. I don't know what's to become of you. Sometimes I think you're not all there . . ."

"Ma," I said, "will you tell Grandpa something?"

"What is it now?" Her voice dripped with suspicion.

"Ma, we have to have his telescope."

There was a moment of silence as heavy as lead.

"Did I hear you right? You said 'telescope'?"

"Ja," I said. "Telescope."

"You haven't got some crazy idea again—like hunting lost treasure or something like that?"

"No, honest, Ma," I said. "We just want it."

"What on earth for?"

"We're going to study nature," I said. I figured I didn't have to tell her it was human nature we were planning to study.

She just sighed. "Poor Aunt Lou," she said. "All right. I'll tell him. When do you need it?"

"As soon as he comes out. After all, we can't stay long. School will be starting."

"At least you've got that in mind," said Mother. "That's something. I'll just send your rubbers and raincoat along. And your geometry book. Grandpa'll probably drive out that way in the morning. He said he was going to the mill, and he won't mind going a little farther if he goes that far."

She rang off.

I went back out to the porch. Everybody looked expectantly at me. "He'll bring it tomorrow," I said.

"Well, that's settled," said Great-aunt Lou. "Now I'd better be gettin' back to my dishes."

She got up and went into the kitchen.

Great-uncle looked at me quizzically. "You got yourself into something, Old Timer. You'd oughta know better'n to cotton up to a woman."

"Oh, I don't know," I said. "Sim and I are pretty good at detecting. Look how we outwitted those counterfeiters at Bogus Bluff!"

Sim almost choked. We had got away by the skin of our teeth, just about—no credit to us—and he hadn't forgotten it yet. He still blamed me, and right now he glared at me to remind me.

"Oh, yas, oh, yas," said Great-uncle Joe with fine sarcasm. He pulled himself to his feet. "Time I was gittin' to work. Old Timer, you take Sim around and show him the place before it gits dark. I'll go lend Burl a hand."

"I'll come along," said Gus.

I took Sim around, showed him the barn and the hay-loft, with the corn-sheller in it, and the pig-pen. I showed him the corn cribs, the machine shed, the place where Great-uncle Joe kept the car and the surrey and the wagon. I took him up a little slope west of the house to a round hilltop without many trees on it, so he could look around and see the Fair Valley Store south of us, and Gus Elker's and Stone's on the other side, and Ed Burke's, and over on the eastern sky, the grand Ortell house on top of the Mill Bluff.

He never said a word until I pointed to the Mill Bluff. Then he said, "That's next to the pond we were going to fish when we got here."

"Ja," I said. "Only we didn't get to go."

"Don't I know it!" He made a derisive sound. "You and your promises. I should have known better."

He didn't say anything else, but I could tell he was thinking plenty. When the right time came, he'd open up with it, too. It made me feel uncomfortable.

We set out down the hill for the house. The whippoorwills were calling a little—not much; they never called much in August, usually only a short while half an hour after sundown—and the stars were coming out. And what an evening it was for stars! There were four evening stars, as bright as could be. Venus and Jupiter were the brightest, then Mars, then Saturn. There they all were.

"You don't often see four planets at once," I said.

"Right about now I'd sooner see a fat bass at the end of my line," said Sim.

"Heck!" I said, "we've got two weeks to fish!"

"You know what I think?" said Sim. "I think we'll be lucky if we get any time at all to go fishing."

Sim always looked on the dark side of everything. It was his nature; he couldn't help it. I held my tongue because I was afraid to say what I wanted to say for fear Sim would get so mad he'd decide to go home and set out for Sac Prairie on foot.

"Don't it smell nice?" I said after a while.

"Uh-huh," he said.

It did, too. Hay smell was in the air, and the musk of corn, and the freshness of the river and the marshes, and the hot summer smell of woods filled with oak trees and soft maples, every leaf of which was giving off perfume to the summer night. It smelled of Great-aunt Lou's bergamotte and sweet basil, of sage and thyme, of mint geranium.

Great-aunt Lou had just finished cleaning up when we got back to the house. Her dishes were put away, and she was taking up some patching, while her old black cat was purring around her ankles.

"We're going up to unpack," I said.

"Take that lamp over on the sewing-machine, boy," she said.

I took the lamp, lifted the chimney, and lit it. Sim gave me a sidelong glance.

Great-aunt Lou caught it with her sharp eyes. She smiled. "We never put the electricity in upstairs," she said.

"Most of the farms around here don't have it yet," I said. "Come on."

Sim followed me upstairs into the attic. The little lamp made a cozy glow there. It was easily enough to read by. Great-aunt Lou had been in and turned down the bed. She had opened the gable windows, and the night wind was flowing through, drawing in all the fragrance from outside.

Sim sat down on the bed. His face was as set as a stone. "I don't know how I let you get me into this," he said. "For a fact, I don't. Here I could have been fishing all afternoon. Then you came and Pa said, 'Go!' and Ma said it was all right. I guess I'm just a jellyfish. No mind of my own!"

I gave him a sarcastic laugh. "No mind of your own!" I hollered. "Listen! If everybody had as much mind of their

own as you've got, the world'd be made up of bullheads!
You're the orneriest, stubbornest cuss in Sac Prairie, and
you glory in it. You're out here because you couldn't resist.
You were afraid you'd miss something. You're afraid you're
missing something at home now. That's all that's eating
you. You had a big supper, you've got a nice soft bed, and
we've got two weeks to loaf around in."

"I didn't hear any plans to loaf," said Sim dryly. "I ob-
serve, as usual, you talk too much. You opened right up to
give Gus Elker an assist. It was a wonder to me you waited
as long as you did to butt in."

"I was just being helpful."

"Ha! I can see it. Your head was filling up with visions
of playing detective."

"Sim," I said, "what do you think?"

"I don't know Jake Riley," he answered. "I don't know
Gus Elker."

"Do you think there's something in it?"

"I guess there could be. It sounds queer, all right. And
it makes me kind of nervous. You're no shining light, but
you've got a real talent for getting a person into trouble."

"That's the nicest thing you've said to me all day," I
said. I meant it, too.

He grinned. "We'll see how it turns out."

"I can hardly wait," I said.

"Truer words were never spoke!" he answered. "It's
written all over you."

4.

We Become Irregulars

GRANDFATHER ADAMS came with the telescope early next morning. I could see when he looked at Sim and me sitting on the back porch steps as he got the telescope out of the car and came over that he was pretty doubtful about giving it to us.

"Now what's up?" he asked. "Can't be star-gazing. You get to do enough of that at home. I thought you were bent on fishing."

"So did I, Mr. Adams," said Sim.

I told him.

He began to laugh. "Great God in Heaven!" he cried. "My boy, that Great-uncle of yours together with Gus Elker can hatch up the dandiest fooferaws in the county. What does your Great-aunt say about it?"

"She sort of goes along with it," I said.

Grandfather raised his eyebrows. He took out a cigar, clipped it, and lit it. He puffed at it thoughtfully, one hand in his pocket, the other holding his cigar.

"What could it be about, Grandpa?" I asked.

"Isn't that your job?" he wanted to know. "Aren't you

the great reader of detective stories? You know all about Sherlock Holmes and Dr. Fu Manchu and Dr. Thorneyke —I don't. But let me give you some advice—go slow."

"Grandpa, I always take my time," I said.

"You go at everything like a bull in a china shop. Except work. And stay out of caves," added Grandfather.

Sim burst out laughing. That was a sore point, ever since we got ourselves trapped in a cave down the river a couple of months before.

"A man who sticks his nose too far into somebody else's business is liable to get it pinched," said Grandfather. He pointed to the telescope. "That's a safe beginning. It'll keep you at a good distance."

"Grandpa, is Jake Riley a bad man?" I asked.

"Well, what's 'bad'?" asked Grandfather. "Nobody's all bad. Nobody's all good. I'd say everybody's a little of both —some more one side, some the other. Jake's no saint, as far as I know. Ask your Grandfather Grendon—he's attended him when he was under the weather."

"He's not here," I said. "And I can't ask him on the telephone. It's a party line, and everybody listens."

Grandfather Adams chuckled. "Curiosity is inveterate in all the animal kingdom," he said.

Great-uncle Joe came riding down into the farmyard on the hay-rake. He had been windrowing hay. The moment he caught sight of Grandfather Adams, he let out a shout.

"You on the loose again, Adams?" he hollered as he jumped off the seat and started toward us.

"I keep trying to find an odder specimen of the local fauna than you, Joe," said Grandfather. "So far, I haven't been able to do it."

Great-uncle wasn't sure whether he had been insulted or not. "They don't grow people like me all over, Adams," he said.

"Thanks to the mercy of Providence!" answered Grandfather. "Now tell me, Joe—what's this about Jake Riley?"

"Wish I could tell you," answered Great-uncle. "Trouble is, I don't know. He's actin' mighty queer, is all, and the boys has decided to do a little snoopin' around. I don't care much, myself, as long as Molly don't come to harm, but Gus Elker—why, ever since he was 'lected Justice of the Peace, he's taken it into his head he's responsible for all the laws in the books."

Grandfather Adams smiled. "I see."

What he saw was plain. He was convinced Gus Elker and Great-uncle Joe were off on another wild-goose chase. I wasn't so sure they weren't, myself. Many a time I'd gone along because one or the other got some crazy idea into his head, and it usually took Great-aunt Lou to get us out of the mess Gus and Great-uncle got into.

"I'll tell you, boy," he said, turning to me. "You sit tight till you hear from me. I'll just drive around by way of Skunk Hollow and take a look for myself."

He went into the house to talk with Great-aunt Lou.

"He's too sharp for his own good," said Great-uncle.

"He wants to make sure," said Sim approvingly. "He's being practical." He shot a glance at me. "Some people can let their imaginations run off with 'em."

He couldn't have made it any clearer if he had kicked me.

It took only an hour for Grandfather Adams to telephone.

"Go ahead," he said. "There's something up, all right."

I didn't wait another minute. I grabbed the telescope. "Come on," I said to Sim. "Gus Elker'll show us where to go."

"Be careful now," cautioned Great-aunt Lou.

Sim followed me out through the farmyard, up the pasture lane, and around the barn. We went north along the fence between the cornfield and the pasture, then crossed the line-fence to Gus Elker's land. Gus's house was a low, one-storey house, with a long back porch facing south. His dogs set up such a barking as we came down toward them, that Gus showed up in the doorway of his toolshed.

I just waved at him and hollered. "We're ready, Gus. Show us where to go."

Gus launched himself toward us in a funny kind of running gait, as if he were crouched for a cross-country race. He was breathless by the time he got across that short distance to us.

"Jukas! What's all the hurry?" he wanted to know.

"Grandpa brought out the telescope," I said. "Here it is."

"Lemme see. Lemme take a look through it," said Gus eagerly.

Sim began to snicker. I took the telescope out of its case and opened it up. Gus turned it squarely on the house, which was about twenty feet away.

"Can't see a thing," he announced. "Always said them new-fangled inventions wasn't worth much."

I took hold of him and turned him so he could look over toward the Ortell house.

"That's better," he said. "I can see a hawk settin' right up there. I be dog if he don't seem right over there. If I got my gun . . ."

"He'd be over in Dane County by the time you got within shooting range," I said. "That's enough now. Let's go."

Gus surrendered the telescope reluctantly, and led the way, mumbling to himself, out of the yard. "Kids ain't what they used to be," he said. "I like to die if I so much as opened my mouth to my Pa."

"Kids are all the same, Gus," I said. "Grandpa Adams says so."

"Well, he knows ever'thin'," said Gus sarcastically.

I thought any minute his overalls were going to fall off of him. Sim looked goggle-eyed at the way they flapped around him and billowed out in the west wind. Gus was heading northeast. He skirted the fields and came to the edge of an oak woods. There he stopped.

"Ain't no use me goin' on," he said. He pointed ahead. "You git along through this here woods an' up on the ridge. That there farm down in the Pocket is Jake's. Can't miss it. It's dead ahead, straight as the crow flies. It's the only farm in Skunk Hollow that ain't square on the road."

"We'll find it," I said.

Gus looked doubtful. He stood for a moment irresolute. He took off his felt hat and scratched his touseled head. Then he put his hat on again and looked at us sadly, shook his head, and walked back the way we had come.

"You lug this a-while," I said to Sim, offering him the telescope.

"That was your idea alone," said Sim. "It's your responsibility. If something happens to it, I won't pay for it."

"Okeh, okeh," I said. "I'll pay for it."

He took the telescope and we went on.

We reached the top of the ridge, finally. Even though the wind was blowing strong now, the August afternoon was hot. There were only a few clouds in the sky, and they seldom crossed the sun. In addition to the heat, deer flies pestered us.

We went low along the south side of the ridge, so we wouldn't be seen from the valley below, until we were just opposite Jake Riley's farm. The house and barn lay at the head of a pocket, well back from the Skunk Hollow road east of it—about half a mile, I judged. There were fields all around the buildings, but most of the worked land was east and northeast of the house because the ridge on which we stood divided to the west, and one part of it ran in a curving line around the buildings into the north and northeast all the way to the Witwen road and the creek that flowed down to the millpond east of Ortell's Bluff. Thus there were woods on three sides.

We picked a place where a big old oak tree divided just about at the base, so we could put the telescope in between the trunks and lie there looking down. We were just in line with the house there.

"You first," I said to Sim, inviting him to look.

He shook his head. "I'm too hot from that long walk. I'll just sit here and cool off—if the flies'll let me." He snorted. "You and the country!"

I lay down in the grass, never minding the twigs and last year's acorns scattered there, and adjusted the telescope. I could see everything around the house—the chickens moving, Jake's two cows, a few ducks, a fat old turkey, a dog wallowing in the cool ground in the shade of an old box-elder tree east of the house. But not a sign of Jake—

or Molly. The house faced east, and the porch was in plain sight; nobody sat on it. It must have been mighty hot in that house because the sun shone on most of it. I looked at the second-storey windows; Molly's room, Great-aunt Lou had said, was in the southeast corner. I couldn't see any movement there, either, and I could even look partly into the room.

Behind me, Sim began to mutter. I figured it was about time for him to boil over.

"This is just about the craziest thing we ever did," said Sim. "I don't know for a fact how I got talked into it."

"You said that before," I said.

"Sitting here in the woods with the ants crawling over us and the deerflies making life miserable and once in a while a mosquito sinking his shaft into us when we could be down behind the Electric Theatre pulling in sunfish or rock bass. You don't call this sane. Like your Ma says, you must be out of your mind." Sim spoke bitterly. He was having visions of pulling in fish as we never pulled them in before.

I didn't say anything.

"What do you see?" he asked.

"What'd you expect I'd see in two minutes? Jake Riley coming out in plain sight and committing a murder, or something? You have to be patient."

"Nobody can say I haven't been patient," said Sim. "I'm beginning to think I'm the one who's not in his right mind."

"That's a proposition I won't argue with," I said.

I shifted the telescope a little. There was nobody in the fields, either, unless they were among the corn-rows. The corn was in bloom. Now and then I could smell the rich musk of the blossoms way up here on the ridge.

I moved the telescope higher in the crotch and held it, turning it on the other farms in Skunk Hollow. I could look all the way to where the Witwen road went by north of the Hollow, a dusty line against the marshland beyond. There were people moving around everywhere at the other farms.

I looked back at Riley's. Nothing but the animals could be seen.

I backed away from the telescope and sat up. "There's nothing moving there except chickens," I said. "You want to look?"

But Sim was already looking at something. He was gazing up past the farm, into the woods on the ridge leading toward the Witwen road.

"I wonder if we're the only ones watching Jake Riley's," he said.

I tried to look where he looked. I could see only the woods, hot and green under the sun.

"You take and line up that telescope about one degree northeast of the lightning-rod on Riley's barn," said Sim, "and raise her about up to the top of the ridge, not quite. Now and then something up there glints and shines. Two spots."

I picked up the telescope, bringing it up along one tree trunk. I got the lightning-rod into line. I saw leaves and trees—plenty of them. Oak trees, hard maples, some birch.

"Maybe it's quartz," I said. "That shines."

"It's not quartz."

Suddenly I caught something shining, too. I couldn't make it out.

"There it was," Sim said.

"I know. But the wind blew a branch back over it," I said. "From here, the branch is in line. When the wind blows, the sun hits whatever it is, and we get a glimpse of it."

I lowered the telescope slowly, bringing it down inch by inch. I saw cloth and a man's shoe.

"There *is* someone there," I said. "I can see a leg."

"Binoculars?"

"Can't see that. The branch is in the way. He's got on blue serge pants. Now, wait, let me see. He's moving his foot," I said, watching the shoe. "He's somebody from town. He's got on leather-soled shoes. Nobody from the country'd go into hills with leather soles and slip all around."

"Let me look."

I backed away. Sim came down to one knee and put his eye to the telescope.

"A greenhorn," said Sim. "That's a good pair of pants, and that hill's full of prickly ash."

"A city fellow."

Sim sat back, letting the telescope go to the crotch again. He leaned against the tree and sat cross-legged, facing me. His lean face showed how puzzled he was.

"Who's crazy now?" I asked.

"It don't add up," he said thoughtfully. "Let's say Jake Riley's got his stepdaughter locked up. All right, so far. Then what's that fellow over there got to do with it? Watching the house."

"Maybe she's got a beau and he's come out to keep an eye on her," I said. "He's going to rescue her . . ."

Sim interrupted me sarcastically. "That's what comes of reading that novel by Ruby M. Ayres. I remember when you talked Miss Mergan into letting you have it from the library. *The Scar*."

"You don't know the first thing about romance," I said.

"I know just enough to figure out there's no way she'd get to know a city fellow," said Sim scornfully. "And a fine lot of rescuing he'd do from way up there on the hill. What a greenhorn he'd have to be, too, to watch the house from that side, with the sun hitting those glasses . . ."

"He came in from the Witwen road," I said. "He must have."

Sim went back to the telescope and moved it along the Witwen road. "He'd have to walk it, then. There's no car in sight."

"It could be parked behind the hill at the peaviner," I said. "But more likely he's got somebody coming to pick him up later on."

"That could be," admitted Sim, reasonably enough. "A parked car'd sure draw attention out here in the country. But it don't add up."

It didn't either, any way I could figure it. Molly was close to eighteen. From what Great-aunt Lou had said, she never got out much. Not even to the County Fair in Baraboo.

Sim turned back to the telescope and looked again.

"He's gone now," he said, after a while.

He moved the telescope around, looking over the hillside across from us. Then he turned it back to the house.

"There," he said suddenly, "is that a hand inside the window?"

I shoved him aside and looked into Molly's bedroom. Sure enough, I could see a slim white hand and part of an arm dangling over the edge of the bed.

"Maybe he's killed her," I said excitedly.

"That'd be some place to keep a corpse," said Sim, chuckling. "On the bed. You've got too much imagination."

"She moved her hand."

"There goes your corpse," said Sim scornfully.

Down in the valley, Jake Riley came out on the porch. He was a fat man, very fat. He had three chins, none of them shaved. His hair was thin on top, thick on the sides of his head. He had bushy eyebrows, just beginning to gray. His mouth was thick and coarse, and his nose was broad. His arms were wide and fat, and his hands were like small hams. He sat in a rocker on the porch and fanned himself.

"Jake's out," I said, watching. "Now he's eating an apple, core and all. Just four bites. No wonder he's so fat!" There was a flash of white in the doorway behind Jake. "It's Molly," I cried.

"There's a car driving up from the Skunk Hollow road," said Sim.

"Ja. He sees it," I said. "He's sending her back in."

Jake Riley's face was dark and angry. He pushed Molly back into the house. She looked scared. I saw her pass through the kitchen. Then she was back in her room; she crossed the window and vanished.

The car came just part way up the lane, then backed out again. The driver had got onto the wrong road, that was all. As soon as he saw he was on a driveway, not the road, he turned around.

Jake just kept on sitting there.

"I guess that settles that," I said. "He's keeping her penned up. Gus was right."

"But what for?" asked Sim.

"That's the next step," I said. "To find out. Are you game now?"

"I'm game," said Sim.

We shook on it. "We're in the detective business," I said. "We might not be as good as Sherlock Holmes—but we can do as much as his Baker Street Irregulars. We're Irregulars—we're the Mill Creek Irregulars!"

5.

Our Detective Kit

A T THE dinner table that noon I told what we had seen.
"We could watch day after day," I said, "and
chances are we wouldn't find out much more. It surely looks
as if he's got Molly kept in her room. He just lets her out
when nobody's around—that's the way it looks. Somehow
we have to get into that house."

"We gotta obey the law," said Gus Elker, who had come
over to sit in.

"Sure, sure—till the horse is stole," said Great-uncle.

"I on'y know what I read in the law-books," said Gus,
aggrieved.

Great-uncle looked suddenly secretive. "All I know is—
things is happenin' hereabouts. I seen me a stranger myself
this morning—up on the hill west a the house."

Gus said something and Great-aunt Lou said something,
and I looked at Sim and jerked my head toward the back
porch. I went out and he followed.

"Listen," I said, "what's going on here's more than just
Jake Riley locking up his stepdaughter."

48

"Ah," said Sim, "you've been making deductions. If you're so all-fired smart, what is it?"

"I don't know. But I'll tell you what. We'll need to detect in earnest," I said. "You remember that stuff I gave you the time I got it from the mail-order detective school?"

Once, when I had given up the idea of being a pianist and composer, and before I thought that being a writer was just about the easiest way of making a living I knew, I had made up my mind to be a detective—like Sherlock Holmes or Father Brown or Lecoq. That was after I gave up the idea of becoming a lawyer.

"You mean all that fingerprinting stuff?"

"Sure," I said. "You still got it? We might need it."

"It's in the office somewhere."

Sim had an "office" behind the harness shop. He kept everything in it—tools, fishing paraphernalia, sporting magazines, all the files of his old enthusiasms.

He started to laugh. "Fingerprints!" he said. "Sometimes your imagination just sweeps you off your feet."

"Laugh," I said. "I know what I'm talking about."

"We've got to give this a good think. We don't want to rush in."

"Well, while you're thinking, I'll get into town somehow and dig up that fingerprinting set and all," I said. "If you'll tell me where to look."

The idea of somebody pawing around in his office horrified Sim. "I'll go along," he said quickly.

I marched back into the kitchen and announced that we had to go into town, we had forgotten something.

"Well, the walkin's easy," said Great-uncle, his large frame shaken by laughter at his little joke.

"I expect to walk it," I said, with as much dignity as I could muster in the face of seven miles of dusty road afoot.

Gus Elker spoke up. "I have to drive in today. I can take the boys."

Great-aunt Lou looked at me quizzically. She had a pretty good idea that something was going on, but she said nothing. Her look was enough.

Gus didn't tell us why he was going to Sac Prairie, but we soon found out. It was stock day. On stock day a lot of farmers came into town with cattle, calves, and pigs, to load them into the stock cars of the Milwaukee Road on a siding just a block or so down the street from where we lived. On this particular day Gus had a load of pigs to take into town.

Gus had not long before bought himself a truck in place of the deep wagon-box he had used before, and he wasn't quite sure of himself yet. So he drove just the opposite of Great-uncle Joe; he just crawled along. We were all crowded into the one seat, the pigs were squealing and bellowing because they were more crowded than we were, the day was hot, and the smell of those pigs just rode right along with us and all the dust.

I thought that ride would never end.

Gus went into town by way of the Lower Mill Road, and turned right up toward the depot, near which the stock-yards stood. The animals would have to be unloaded here and weighed before they could be put into the cars—and they were never loaded into the cars until just before the train pulled out. There were three or four farmers ahead of Gus; so he would be busy awhile.

"We'll meet you down town," I said to Gus, as we got out of his truck. "At Jones' Harness Shop."

Gus just nodded and went off to join the other farmers.

"Whew!" said Sim, once we were away from the stock-yards. "I'm glad to get out of there."

"It's mostly ammonia," I said. "You ought to know. You're taking chemistry—I'm not."

"I don't care what it's mostly, I still don't like it. Now where you going? I thought we were heading for the office."

"Seeing as how we're so close to home," I said, "I thought we'd just run up home and see if Ma baked anything."

We went up along the depot platform, waving at Mr. Porter, the station-agent, who sat inside before the tele-graph key with his green shade over his eyes. We could hear the key clicking. We ran over the crossroads, past the grain elevator, and up the street into the house.

Mother had baked, all right. Fresh coffeecake and a roly-poly, which was just coffeecake rolled up with lots of raisins inside. My sister was the only one in the house when we came in, and the minute she saw me grab a knife and head for the roly-poly, she started to holler.

"Ma! Ma! Steve's cutting the coffeecake," she called out.

Mother appeared in the doorway of the summer-kitchen and came flying toward the house.

"What are you doing home?" she cried.

"They just got hungry and came home," said my sister.

Right there I made a mistake. I said, "We just came for my fingerprint outfit—I gave it to Sim. We're going to get it."

Mother's eyes kind of crinched up. "Fingerprinting!"

she cried. "Stephen, what are you doing out there? Are you pestering Aunt Lou and Uncle Joe?"

"No, Ma—honest," I said.

No matter how earnest I was, Sim spoiled it. He looked as guilty as if we had just robbed the Farmers & Citizens Bank, and still had all the money in our pockets.

"Stephen, we'll just have to come to an understanding," said Mother, standing there with her mouth as firm as a rock. She was getting excited, and she always looked more handsome and pretty when she was upset, only I never appreciated it.

"How come you always act as if I were a criminal?" I hollered. "I'm innocent. I haven't done a thing. What could a boy do out there on the farm in the middle of the woods?"

"You'd never have to think twice about getting into trouble," my sister said.

"You shut up," I said.

"Stephen! Don't raise your voice so. What will the neighbors think?"

"There's Mrs. Mulrooney on the porch," said my sister helpfully.

Mother always thought a lot about what the neighbors might think. She really worried about it. Grandfather Adams laughed at her, Father laughed at her, and while I didn't dare laugh at her, I laughed at the neighbors.

"I'm not accusing you of anything," said Mother quietly. "I'm only asking to make sure."

"Okeh," I said. "I'm not up to anything you have to worry about."

"All right, then," said Mother, who was looking nervously out the window toward the Mulrooney house, afraid

Mrs. Mulrooney had already heard me hollering. "Go along with you, then. You might as well wrap up the rest of that roly-poly and take it along," she added. "There's hardly enough left to put on the table."

"Gee, thanks," I said.

I did it. She leaned down for me to kiss her cheek, I wrinkled my nose at my sister, and got out the back door before Mother could think of something else to ask about.

"Your mother's a wonderful woman," said Sim, as we crossed the tracks.

"I know it," I said. "Only, I wouldn't dare tell her—it might go to her head, and then there'd be no living with her."

At the harness shop, Old Fred looked at us as if he couldn't believe his eyes. "My gosh! Look what the cat dragged in," he said, when he found his voice. "Ain't you boys lost?"

"Not yet," I said. "We're on a raid."

"They surely feed you well enough out there," said Fred.

"It takes more than food, Mr. Jones," I said. "You said it yourself—birds and animals and all."

Old Fred kept one eye on Sim. He saw Sim get the keys for his office. He looked over at me and smiled.

"Come on," said Sim.

We went out to his office. Oh, it was hot and stuffy in there! It had been closed for a long time and smelled of magazines, old papers, and a lot of things I couldn't identify—leather, perhaps, Sim's old rubber boots for minnow-seining, and so on. The detective kit was somewhere in all that stuff.

But Sim had a pretty good idea where it was, and he

found it after only five minutes. The only difference in it was that now everything was in order, and it hadn't been when I gave it to him. It was all there—fingerprint pad, paper, ink, disguises, a handbook of clues—we already had plenty of them, I figured—a pair of handcuffs for when we actually caught somebody, and a little gadget you put in your mouth to disguise your voice.

Sim locked up the office and went back to the harness shop. He carried the kit carefully under his arm, trying to hide it from Old Fred. But his father had had plenty of time to get next to Sim. He just sort of gave us a casual glance when we came in through the back door again and chuckled.

"So now it's detecting," he said. "Last June it was exploring for gold. What're you after now?"

"Mr. Jones, it may be a desperate criminal," I said.

"Sure, sure," said Old Fred. "It's no fun if it ain't a desperate criminal. Now, say, I got an old bear-trap out back somewheres—might be you could use that."

Sim ground his teeth and said, "Don't pay no attention to Pa's oil-pouring."

"That's a good idea," I said. "We could set it in the woods and catch that fellow in the blue serge suit . . ."

Sim kicked me, as if to tell me I talked too much.

Old Fred chuckled.

Sim went out the front door of the harness shop. I went after him. We stood on the stoop looking up and down Main Street for sight of Gus Elker. It being stock day, both sides of the street were lined with cars, trucks, and wagons—the high, deep wagons the farmers used for hauling stock. Men and women were moving in and out of the stores.

"A fine detective you'd make," said Sim sarcastically. "When I get back to work, I'm going to make a bridle that'll fit your tongue. Pa catches everything."

"Oh, I know Old Eli's sharp as a needle," I said. "But he's *safe*."

Sim couldn't deny that, or else it would make him seem disloyal. He just gave me a disgusted look.

"Gus Elker's nowhere in sight," I said. "I knew it. I'll tell you what, Sim—I'll just go around to Grandpa Grendon's and see what he knows about Jake Riley."

"Go ahead. I'll wait for Gus."

I ran down Water Street to the corner at the bank, then turned west. Grandfather Grendon had his M.D. shingle out about three blocks west of Main Street; his office was in his house. I hoped he wasn't busy, but he was.

I waited for him in the kitchen, where Grandmother Grendon, who was a small woman, usually dressed in dark brown or tan, ladled out some ground-cherry preserve for me, and sat talking about her flowers—how the squills had been that spring and how the mint geranium and sweet basil were doing in this hot weather, and wanting to know whether I had tasted the harvest apples from her tree yet —and I had, because I had filled my pockets when I came in through the yard; they were still bulging with apples.

Grandfather Grendon came out of the office and through the house to the kitchen. He was a heavy-set man, with a firm, square face. He wore a moustache, but it didn't hide his heavy, impressive mouth.

"I thought you were in the country," he said.

"I just came in. Had to get something."

"And you came around to get something to eat," he said. "How many places have you been to? You'll get fatter than you are already."

"Grandpa, I'm not fat," I said indignantly.

"Boy, every fat man who ever lived said the same thing. Didn't change anything."

There was no use arguing with Grandfather Grendon. He always spoke as if he were in the pulpit and God had put the idea right into his mouth.

"Grandpa, do you know Jake Riley?"

"Out in Skunk Hollow?" And, at my nod, "Sure, I know the old reprobate."

My face must have brightened at that, because he eyed me so suspiciously, and made me think how strange it was that everybody seems to be suspecting boys of something most of the time.

"Well, who is he?" I asked. "Is he related to Dr. Riley you used to talk about—the one who moved to Baraboo? Or what?"

"No, he's not. No relation at all. He came from Chicago about eight years ago or so, married Mabel Burns, and settled down—if you can call it that—out on Mabel's farm in Skunk Hollow. I've treated him, though there's nothing much wrong with him that less eating wouldn't cure." His keen eyes bored into me. "Why are you asking, boy?"

"Grandpa, he's acting a little queer. Gus Elker says . . ."

He began to laugh. "Gus Elker's not so firm himself," he said. "A fine man, no doubt of that. There's nothing queer about Jake Riley, though. He's a shrewd old devil. You keep out of his reach. But your uncle's place is on the south side of the ridge," he finished, as if that settled that.

I had finished the ground-cherries and got up. I thought I had better get out of there before Grandfather Grendon got it out of me what was cooking. Grandmother came out of the pantry with a sack of cookies, a jar of ground-cherry preserves, and a loaf of her home-made rye bread.

"If you're going into the country," she said, her eyes twinkling, "you'll get hungry."

Grandfather Grendon whooped. "That boy'll be able to live a month on his fat."

"Jasper," said Grandmother sharply, "he's a growing boy."

"Oh, I'll say he is," said Grandfather, laughing heartily. "He's growing in every direction."

I thanked them both and ran out the back door before he could think over what I had asked him.

Sim was still standing on the harness shop stoop, peering down the street for Gus Elker, when I came in through the rear door.

Old Fred never even looked over his shoulder. He was sniffing up his Asthmador; the green smoke curled all over the shop and was being drawn toward the front door. "Where you been all my life?" he asked. "The boy's been chomping on his bit."

"I know it," I said. "He always is."

"I'll bet that old coot forgot us," said Sim, when I came out.

Sim was right, too. When Gus Elker drove up fifteen minutes later, he said sheepishly, "I be dog if I wasn' half way out to the mill when I recollected you boys." He hollered into the harness shop. "Hello, Fred! Y' git over the Old Settlers' Picnic?" He didn't wait for an answer. "Git in, boys, git in. We'll make time now."

We made time, all right. It took us just about an hour to make the seven miles to the farm.

6.

Sim Scores

Next morning we came face to face with Jake Riley for the first time. Great-uncle Joe had taken us along to Grell's Mill to have some feed ground. All the farmers in the Mill Creek country brought their grain to the mill, and most of the time shopped in the store just north of the mill.

Six or seven farmers were there before Great-uncle, their wagons or trucks drawn up in a half circle before the old mill, which rose up beside the pond. Its wheel was covered, but the sound of the water at the wheel washed steadily into the sunny morning. Great-uncle got right out of his truck and started to talk to Ed Burke about their dogs.

Sim and I got out, too. Nobody paid much attention to us. We wandered into the mill, which was full of grain dust. It was pretty much like the grain elevator in Sac Prairie, except that this mill was a lot older, almost eighty years old; it had been standing here a long time, and it was nice to hear the water turning the old wheel; its voice came up sort of like the pulse of the mill.

There was a loading platform along the road side of the

mill, and we came out to it just as a battered old truck drove up. Great-uncle Joe looked away from Ed Burke and down to the truck, and his face kind of pulled together.

I looked, too. I grabbed Sim by the arm.

"It's Jake Riley," I said. "And he's got Molly with him."

The fat man got out of the car backwards; if he'd have tried it frontwards, he'd have lost his balance. He leaned back into the car and said something hard to Molly. She didn't answer, just sat there. He came on up the steps to the loading platform. He walked with his feet out, pointing away from him, sideways, sort of hitching along. He had a wide-brimmed hat on; it shaded his face and made him look dark-skinned. The wind worked in the thick hair on the side of his head. He was shaved this morning, and sunlight gleamed on his chins.

Great-uncle turned to face him as he mounted the platform. "Ain't seen you for a coon's age, Jake," he said. "W'ere you been keepin' yourself?"

"Been home," said Jake shortly.

He had a voice like a bear's growl. If he meant to tell my Great-uncle by the sound he made that he didn't want to talk, Great-uncle didn't let on he heard him.

"How you keepin' busy on that big farm a your'n?" he asked, grinning. 'My ol' woman, she's been sayin' she's missed seein' you and Molly."

Jake took a toothpick out of his pocket and stuck it into his mouth to chew at it. "Been meaning to come over," he said. "You know how it is."

"Watch me," I whispered to Sim.

I went over and stood in front of Jake Riley. "Mister," I said, "how come a man can get so fat?"

He took the toothpick out of his mouth and stared at me. It wasn't an unfriendly look; it wasn't friendly, either. It was just cold. Then he grinned, and all three of his chins grinned with him. He stuck a fat finger into my belly.

"Boy," he said, "with the start you got, you're going to find out."

"Don't pay no attention to him," said Great-uncle hastily.

"He belongs with you?" asked Jake.

"My niece's boy. He's stayin' with us for a spell."

"He has a little of Jasper Grendon's look," said Jake reflectively.

"Should have," said Great-uncle. "The boy's his grandson. Old Timer, git out a the man's way."

"He's not in my way," said Jake. He just reached out and brushed me aside like a twig.

I sat down on the dusty floor of the platform. I was too surprised to say anything. Everybody was laughing, but I just sat and looked up at Jake Riley. He was sort of smiling, but his eyes were hard. They were like pools of gray water with flecks of ice in them.

He stood for only a minute or less; then he went into the mill. I got up and dusted off my pants before I went back to where Sim still stood.

He was grinning. "I watched you," he said. "I don't figure you could have done anything plain dumber."

"How so?" I demanded.

"Why, the reason the Baker Street Irregulars could be so useful is that they weren't noticed," he said. "And here you go, first thing, and get yourself noticed good."

I didn't say anything. There was nothing to say. Sim was right and I was wrong. I looked around, but by this time everybody seemed to have forgotten me. Everybody—but Molly Burns. She sat stone still in the truck with one hand pressed against her lips and her eyes fixed right on me.

I walked down the platform steps and over to Jake Riley's truck. I stopped beside Molly Burns.

"You all right?" I asked.

"Are *you* all right?" she said. "I saw him knock you down."

"Aw, that was nothing," I said.

"Old Timer!" Great-uncle Joe called. "Be careful now."

I could see he was afraid I'd blurt out something. "Don't worry about me," I hollered. "I don't figure she can knock me over as easy as he did."

Everybody laughed again. Except Molly.

She leaned forward and pointed at Great-uncle Joe. "Are you related to Mr. Stoll?"

"He's my great-uncle."

"And Mrs. Stoll's your aunt, then," she said, sort of fast. Her eyes began to sparkle and she began to look excited, just as if she were playing a game and it was her chance to score.

"Are you sure," I said, "you're all right?"

The minute I said it, the sparkle went out of her eyes, and her face just grew set. But she wasn't looking at me. She was looking over me, toward the mill. I turned. Jake Riley was coming slowly down the steps.

"Come, girl," he said to Molly. "We'll just leave the truck and go over to the store."

Molly got down out of the truck without a look at me or Sim and went alongside Jake Riley toward the Mill Creek Store. You would never have guessed that anything could be wrong, but I was more sure than ever that something was. I watched them vanish inside the store.

"Old Timer," called Great-uncle. When I glanced up, he tossed me half a dollar. "Go to the store and git me a pound of Plowboy," he said.

I caught the half dollar and headed for the store. Sim was right at my heels.

The Mill Creek Store was set back from the road far enough so cars and buggies could park a good way off the highway. It was about halfway back toward the edge of the millpond. Like all the other stores at Witwen and Black Hawk and Leland and Denzer, it was crammed from floor to ceiling with just about everything you'd want to buy. There was an open cracker-barrel—that was what Sim headed for right away—and right next to it, a box of fig-bars. Eggs stood in baskets on the counter near the scales and a big old coffee-grinder. Open sacks of potatoes were ranged along the counter in the narrow aisle on one side, and on the other were piles of overalls and shirts and all kinds of clothing. The shoes were on shelves in one corner, and groceries and some dry goods were on the other shelves. Hardware and rubber boots hung from hooks in the ceiling, except down over the aisles and at the rear end of the store, where there were four or five captain's chairs around a cold stove for the neighborhood loafers to sit. Mr. Reible and his wife, who ran the store, were always kept busy. I knew them both, because I used to go into the store when I came out to fish in the pond with Grandfather Adams or went on his rounds with Grandfather Grendon.

The minute I stepped into the store, I shot a quick glance around for Jake Riley and his stepdaughter. They were buying groceries. While Sim headed for the cracker-barrel, I went up to the counter and beckoned to Mr. Reible, who came right over.

"I want a pound of Plowboy," I said.

"Ain't you a little young for tobacco?" he asked, when he gave it to me.

"It's for Great-uncle Joe," I said.

"That's what all the boys say," he answered, and walked away chuckling and shaking his head, acting as if he really believed I wanted that stuff for myself.

I looked around as much as I could, trying to keep an eye on Jake Riley and Molly Burns. But there were too many people in the store, and they milled around too much. I couldn't just up and follow them around. I couldn't even keep track of Sim. The store was crowded without any people at all in it, and now it seemed packed with not more than ten people in it. I knew if I stood much longer, I'd be drawing attention to myself. So I went outside and waited there for Sim.

He came in a few minutes. He was carrying something carefully in a sack.

"You bought something," I said.

"My, that's a smart deduction," he said, starting toward the mill.

"What'd you buy?" I asked. "It's too big a bag for candy and as long as you got the crackers free, it's a cinch you wouldn't buy them."

"Go on," he said. "You're nowhere near hot."

"I could always take the sack and look in," I said.

"I bought a box of cornstarch," he said.

"Cornstarch!" I hollered. "Well, I see it plain now—I'm not the only hare-brain around."

"No, the world's full of 'em," agreed Sim, with a grin.

I figured Sim must have some reason for buying cornstarch, but I couldn't guess what it was. Sim couldn't cook, outside of frying fish. But he wasn't offering a word of explanation. He just carried that sack on his hands like some kind of treasure. Cornstarch! Why, you couldn't even eat that!

The look of disgust on my face must have been strong enough for Great-uncle Joe to see. As we came up, he asked, "What's the matter, Old Timer?—Jake get away from you?"

"No, he's back there," I said.

Sim dug his elbow into my ribs.

I looked around. Jake Riley and his stepdaughter were almost close enough behind us to overhear what I might have said.

Great-uncle raised his voice. "You git my Plowboy?"

I gave it to him.

"All right, git in," said Great-uncle. "I'm all done. Wasn't anything my old woman wanted from the store?"

"No," I said. "I asked her."

We got into the truck. Great-uncle backed her around and we were off—rattling across the bridge over the millstream, around the bend and over the bridge which crossed the brook below the foaming falls emptying out of the millpond. Sim held that sack as if he had something in it that might spill. Great-uncle looked at him curiously once or twice, but he didn't say anything. Every time the truck tilted a little, Sim juggled that sack around. He held it from the bottom, too, instead of by the neck. Cornstarch! Every time I looked at him he just grinned with that kind of superior look I never saw anybody get on his face as well as Sim.

Since the mill was only around a couple of corners from Great-uncle's farm, we were soon back there. As we rode into the yard, Great-aunt Lou came out of the hen-house. She saw the sack in Sim's hand.

"You boys bought something?" she asked.

"Not I," I said. "Just Sim. Sim's bought you some corn-starch."

"My land to goodness!" Great-aunt almost dropped her apron with the eggs she had gathered in it.

"It's a fact, Mrs. Stoll," said Sim. "And if you'll just lend me a pan to put it in, I'll send it right down."

"It's got a box," I said. "Or did you buy it in bulk?"

"I want the box." Sim refused to be ruffled in the least. He followed Great-aunt Lou into the kitchen, waited until she had disposed of the eggs, then took the pan she gave him and was off up the stairs.

I went after him.

The way he took that box of cornstarch from that sack was enough to make me think he had lost his mind. He picked it up by the corner and put it down the way he'd have handled a thin-shelled egg. He pried the cover off without touching it, dumped the cornstarch into the deep pan Great-aunt Lou had given him, and handed the pan to me.

"There, Steve—you take it down to her," he said. "After all, it was you gave it away."

"You're not mad, are you?" I asked.

"If you mean 'crazy'," he said, "I'm crazy like a fox. If you mean 'angry'—no, I'm not. I wouldn't know what to do with this stuff anyway; so your aunt might's well have it."

I took the pan of cornstarch down to Great-aunt.

"That boy is a little strange," she said. "I declare to goodness!"

"Oh, this is nothing," I said. "You ought to know Sim as well as I do."

The truth was, I was just as puzzled as Great-aunt Lou. Just about everything Sim Jones ever did was as transparent as glass; he was the only one who thought otherwise. Except this. I couldn't figure it out. And if he expected me to climb back up to the attic and stand there with my tongue hanging out till he made up his mind to tell me what he was up to, he had another guess coming.

I went out to the farm buildings and around until I found Great-uncle Joe trying to sew up a bad tear in a binder apron. He cocked his head and looked at me out of his blue eyes and grinned.

"Where's Sim? You and him have a fight?"

I explained that it wasn't that. It was Sim acting so mysterious.

"Well, Old Timer—when you git to be as old as I am, you'll know this world's full of a lot of strange things—and the strangest things on earth is all men, men and women. I never seen anything like the human race. Of course, I ain't been very far out in my life—once down to St. Louis, and once to Chicago, and a couple-a times to Milwaukee—but I figger it that men and women is the same whether you're in England or India or China. It takes a lifetime to figger one human bein' out—and that one's yourself." He cleared his throat and changed his tone. "What were you up to with Jake?"

"I guess I just wanted to show Sim I wasn't afraid of him."

"Old Timer, Jake's a mighty mean man. You take my word for it. Your aunt says he's tetched by the Devil. He set his eye on you good; he'll know you anywheres now. Seems to me the slow way to go about it is the best and safest one."

"I know it," I said, feeling guilty. "I shouldn't have done it."

"The way he pushed you couldn't a hurt you none," said Great-uncle. "You got enough seat to come down on. —Look here, now you ain't spyin' on Jake, jest give me a hand with this here apron. Hold it tight so I can sew it better."

I took hold of the apron and held it taut.

Great-uncle Joe talked steadily as he sewed. He speculated about Jake Riley. He talked about his old friend, Gus Elker. He talked about his brother, my Great-uncle Arnold, who was planning to come up from Spring Green on a visit. He talked about living on the farm, and how different things were twenty years ago.

"Uncle Joe," I said, "it didn't look as if Molly was in much danger. She could've broke and run for it."

He gave me a funny look. "If she had—where'd she a gone? And I don't know how many a them men-folks there might a raised a finger to help her. She's that smart, she knows it. There's something brewin', all right. I seen the look in her face. She's afraid a him, real scared. He's got her buffaloed. Besides—if she wasn't scared—why was she the only one didn't laugh when he upset you? Answer me that!" He shook his head ponderously. "Old Timer, I like to die if she ain't the scaredest girl in Sac County!"

That made sense to me. "But what do we do about it?"

"Seems to me we have to find out first why," he said. "Why is she that scared? She never used to be. It might be a good idea if you got over to look around there after suppertime tonight. I notice he bought a lot of groceries—maybe he's havin' company tonight. Can't tell when the time comes that you'll set eyes on something."

The idea excited me. I let go the apron. "I'll tell Sim," I said.

I ran back to the house, hurried up the stairs, two at a time, and burst into the attic room.

Sim was on his knees, as if he was praying. I couldn't believe it. He hadn't even looked around when I came in. I tiptoed over to where he was and gazed down.

Sim had all our paraphernalia spread out before him, and right square in the middle of it all, tight under a piece of glass, with fixer and dust all around it, was a piece of that cornstarch box.

"There," said Sim, without even looking up, "is a perfect pair of fingerprints—Jake Riley's right thumb and forefinger."

"That's fine," I said, when I found my voice. I meant it, too. "But what do we do with 'em?"

"We'll pass 'em on to Mike Kurth. He's the only policeman we know. And he can find out if these prints are on file anywhere."

He had it all figured out.

7.

Somebody in a Blue Serge Suit

It wasn't until we were on the way up along the ridge above Jake Riley's that evening after supper that I thought of how hard it would be to follow through with Sim's plan. I stopped right where I walked on the path. Sim almost bumped into me.

"Now what?" he growled.

"I just got to thinking," I said. "You know how hard it is to talk to Mike Kurth. You know we could hardly convince him about that counterfeit Liberty-head nickel last June."

The memory immediately darkened Sim's face. Plainly, he hadn't thought about that part of his plan. Besides, he had a horror of law and courts and getting mixed up in anything.

He leaned up against a tree. "We'll have to get somebody else to talk to him. He'll think we're pulling his leg if we come with this so soon after that counterfeit nickel."

"I know it," I said. "But who?"

"Isn't Gus Elker Justice of the Peace? He'd be the one."

"Let's keep him out of it," I said. "If Jake Riley found out—poor Gus wouldn't have a chance."

"That's right," agreed Sim. "But who then?"

The trouble with Mike Kurth was mostly that he was mad at the world of Sac Prairie. The Village Board always tried to take advantage of him, and the kids played all kinds of practical jokes on him. It was no fun for Mike to be Village Marshal, but it was fun for practically everybody else. Just the same, Mike did his best to see to it that Sac Prairie people obeyed the ordinances and the laws. Mike was particularly hard to convince about anything.

I couldn't think of anyone who might approach Mike except Grandfather Adams, and I knew he would lecture me on dodging my responsibilities if I approached him.

"Well, we can't stand here till the sun goes down," said Sim. "We'll think of something."

We went on along the ridge. Up here, we were on top of the world. The sun hanging over the western rim filled the valleys with the soft rose light of the ending day. East of us, the great shadows of the hills stretched out on the fields and pastures that made a patchquilt of greens and tans all the way to Sac Prairie, which gleamed and shone in the late sunlight over toward the eastern horizon, set against the hills rising across the Wisconsin River east of town. High overhead a pair of redtail hawks wheeled and soared, moving up, up with the currents of air, sometimes screaming. In the south, a long, disorderly file of crows was heading in toward the river bottoms, cawing to one another in that kind of talk crows always make. Ovenbirds sang in the deep woods, and veeries, and a wood thrush was beginning to spill his lyric songs in the shadowed places deep in the wooded valleys. A south wind kept the insects away, and the smell of the woods, rising coolly now after the hot day was almost done, filled all the air with the wild sweetness and pungence of places where men seldom walked and the trees were left to grow undisturbed for scores of years. Oh, but it was good to be there! Walking the ridge was like flying, almost, and it made me feel cut away and free from everything except what I wanted to be tied to like home and Mother and Father and Grandfather Adams and all the rest.

A red fox shot across the ridge in front of us. He was going so fast he never saw us. I stopped again.

"Fox," said Sim flatly.

"Sure," I said. "But why was he running like that? He came from the north."

"Somebody in the woods," ventured Sim.

"Must be. If it was dogs after him, we'd hear them."

We stood still, listening.

We heard mice and voles rustling in the leaves. We heard a snake sliding along not far from us. We heard towhees and fox sparrows scratching for food. And all the birds tuning up for their evening songs. But not a footfall, not a dog's bark.

"Maybe," said Sim sarcastically, "he got a good look at Jake."

"That fellow in the blue serge suit," I said.

"Could be," agreed Sim. "Only—what's he doing?"

"Just what we are," I said. "Come on—our tree's not far off now. We'll look around."

We got to the tree and put up our telescope.

I got down and flattened out to look first at Jake Riley's

house. Molly was outside feeding the chickens. I couldn't see Jake. He was probably in the barn milking the cows. Through the kitchen window, I could see the supper dishes stacked on the table. So they didn't have company.

"That means that whatever's to happen isn't due yet," I said to Sim. "That's my guess. Jake's laid in enough supplies for a week."

"Unless company's due tomorrow," said Sim, cancelling out my deduction. "Let me take a look."

I gave my place to him.

The woods all around us now were filled with a rose glow. In open places the sunlight lay in pools red as blood. Down in Jake Riley's fields the meadow larks were singing. Jake's dog was barking, answering other barking dogs further up Skunk Hollow. The wind was dying down, and the rich musk of the woods was stronger. Not a mosquito made the evening miserable.

North along the hills, blue jays screamed. And the crows cawed. I knew that language.

"There's someone in those woods, all right," I said to Sim. "He's moving north. Just listen to the birds!"

"I hear 'em."

I looked down at the Riley place. The shadows of the hills were closing in around the farm now. Molly was out of the yard, and no one was to be seen. The dogs in the Hollow were still barking, and somewhere a cow bellowed.

A car came leisurely down the Skunk Hollow road, went up over the lesser ridge, and disappeared on its way out the south end. After a little while, another car came in from the south. I watched it coming up the Hollow. It turned in at Jake Riley's.

"Who's that?" I asked Sim. "Is it a stranger?"

"Wait till he gets into range," said Sim irritably. Presently he said, "It's a farmer. Here, you look."

I glued my eye to the telescope. I could see Jake's visitor plain. It was only old man Stone. I was disappointed. Old man Stone was as straitlaced as a deacon who took his duties seriously. He was very likely just stopping by on a matter of business, for the road to his place led in from the Witwen road past the north entrance to the Skunk Hollow. I rolled back from the telescope and sat there with my back to the tree.

"We're not getting any place," said Sim.

"Don't complain," I said. "Think of that fellow in the blue serge suit. I'll bet he's been around day after day."

"Ha! Most likely he's just a birdwatcher out from Madison on a bird-count," said Sim.

"It's the long grind that produces the facts," I said. "Not just catching the crook in the end. It's only the end that's exciting—all the rest is plain hard work."

Sim grunted. "It's getting dark. Can you find your way home from here?"

I just nodded. "I'm thinking maybe we'll slip down to Jake's place and keep our ears open," I said, testing Sim.

His eyes widened. "You're crazy as a loon!" he cried. "That dog down there would set up such a racket you couldn't get near the place."

Just as if he had heard us, Jake Riley's dog began to bark frantically. Down in the valley it was already deepening dusk. The sunlight was gone from the hilltops and the pale washed afterglow was pulling down the west. Lights were on in Jake Riley's kitchen—and in Molly's room, too. Old man Stone's car was still in Riley's yard.

What the dog was barking at was another car coming in Jake Riley's drive.

Sim got down to the telescope again, and maneuvered it around.

The car moved up behind old man Stone's, headlights on, stayed there a minute or so, then backed all the way out again.

Sim drew back from the telescope. "All he did," he said, "was lean forward and look at Stone's car."

"Just long enough," I said, " to take his license. What did he look like?"

"I never saw him before. Only—it looked as if he had on a dark blue suit."

I got excited. "Here we are up here, and there he is down there," I said. "It gets my goat. I know we're on to something, but we're just as far from it as if we were back in Sac Prairie!"

"You're the direct one," said Sim. "Why don't you just go down and ask Jake Riley to his face?"

"Don't goad me," I said.

"Think," said Sim, just to rile me. "What would Sherlock Holmes do?"

"You know he'd sit back in his armchair and figure it all out," I said.

"Too bad we didn't bring along an armchair!"

I looked down into the gathering darkness. "Old man Stone's still there. If we could get down close enough to the house—maybe we could hear what they're talking about."

"We couldn't hear a word over the dog's barking," said Sim scornfully. "And you know it."

"We could leave the telescope right here. Nobody'd come near it all night, and it's clear as a bell out; so it won't get rained on. But we'll have to move while we can still see enough to get through the woods."

"You mean it!" said Sim, as if he were just finding that out.

"Of course, I mean it," I said. "We can come in from the north along that cornfield. What wind there is, is from the south. It's with us. The dog won't smell us on the south side of the house, and he'll have a harder time hearing us."

"Steve, if we got caught, it would spoil everything," protested Sim.

I knew if I stood there listening, Sim would dredge up a hundred good reasons why we shouldn't go down near Jake Riley's house. He was the practical one. He always had logic on his side. All I had was imagination. But when it came to talking, it was a draw, and I knew more words than he did.

"Come on," I said.

I turned and began to walk along the ridge toward the lesser ridge that curved north. I never looked back to see whether he was coming. I couldn't bear to witness that awful soul struggle that would show on his face, before he decided which course he didn't want to follow most —staying there without being absolutely sure of the way back to Great-uncle Joe's farm, or coming along and maybe getting caught. Pretty soon I heard his footsteps behind me.

It was getting to be just dark enough to make the going a little difficult. Sim did his best to keep close to me. He was nervous about the sounds of the woods at night—rabbits, raccoons, anything at all making a noise made him jump, not that he was afraid of rabbits and raccoons, but only because he thought every noise might be a snake and snakes gave him the willies. He had read too much about the deadliness of rattlesnakes, and couldn't square the fright it gave him with the fact that our chance of running into a rattler in these woods was about one in ten thousand.

We got around on the north ridge, and up in a line with Jake Riley's farm, when I stopped short. Sim pitched into me.

"What now?" he growled in disgust.

"Shut up," I whispered, and pointed ahead of us.

A skunk was crossing the route we were taking. Sim just froze. It was a lucky thing I had seen the white stripe down her back in time. I could feel Sim's tenseness; he didn't let out his breath until the skunk had ambled past.

"That was close," he said in relief.

"Skunks usually give warning," I said. "They don't like to use up their musk any more than we like to have it used. I didn't want to surprise her."

We began to drop down the slope toward Jake Riley's cornfield. We were more careful now that we were drawing nearer to the house. The lights in the kitchen and Molly's room were still on, and someone had switched on the yard light in addition. The corn smell came out to meet us. The musk was almost overpowering. Some of the late corn had begun to blossom, and the sweetness was cloying; it seemed to fall upon us and cling to us like dew. It was so strong that it drowned out everything else; the pollen carried it and the leaves breathed it where they rustled in the soft evening wind.

We made our way along the edge of the cornfield up a gentle slope north of the buildings. Overhead the sky was still a little light, not yet dark enough for night. The time of the month was in the dark of the moon, but the planets shone bright in the west and southwest, and one or two stars were already out. But in the valley it was dark; the hills closed in Jake Riley's farm on three sides, and over across the Skunk Hollow road by less than half a mile the Mill Bluff shut off more of the sky.

When we came up even with the barn, I paused to look over the ground. I figured it would be easy to cross to the barn. Once there, I could edge around between the corn-crib and the barn on the side nearest the house. That was in shadow, too, for the yard light was on the pole away from that side of the barn.

"I'm going down," I whispered.

"Don't do it," cautioned Sim. "It'd be just like you to fall over something."

"You go down along the field till you hit the Skunk Hollow road," I said. "Wait for me there."

He stood where he was, one hand on my arm. "If that dog takes out after you, he'll likely have a chunk out of you. You never could run fast."

"I'm more worried about you than you are about me," I said. "Besides, we got Fido at home, and I know all about dogs. I had him hanging on to my seat once when I was swinging. It could've hurt worse."

I pulled away from him and went down to the barn. Looking back, I could make out his dark figure moving off toward the road. He had to skirt another farm to get there, and I hoped he wouldn't forget about the dog there.

I edged around the barn, sort of feeling my way in case anything that rattled—like a milk-pail—might be lying between the barn and the corncrib. My foot touched a board, nothing more. It was loose, and I stepped on it carefully, feeling for nails. I slipped along between the corncrib and the barn, going as far as I could. Over across the pooled glow from the yard light I could see the dog, lying on his side; he seemed to be asleep.

When I had moved forward as far as I thought I dared, I was still too far from the house to hear anything. There I stood. I could see Jake Riley and old man Stone moving around inside the kitchen. Stone was getting ready to go. He was talking vehemently, with many gestures and a lot of nodding and head-shaking, and his face looked angry. Jake just looked half asleep and not troubled at all. But I couldn't hear a word. The closest I came to hearing anything was just the unintelligible sound of their voices— and it was mostly Stone's voice.

Oh, it was maddening! It tantalized me. There I was within a few steps of hearing something that might be important, and I didn't dare move those few steps because the light would show me and the dog would see me and start barking, and Jake would come out and I'd be caught red-handed. I'd never live that down. I couldn't risk it.

But I was just as reluctant to turn back. So I stood where I was. Stood and stood. In the woods the owls began to hoot; their cries echoed across the Hollow. Some cricket frogs still called from up at the creek, and a tree frog or two. Everything else was still.

Then the back door opened, and old man Stone came backing out of the house, as if Jake Riley were pushing him.

"I tell you, Riley, I've waited long enough," Stone was saying, and I could hear it plain, now he was out of the house.

"Patience is a necessary virtue, Mr. Stone," answered Jake, standing in the doorway and just about blotting all the light out of it.

"I've *been* patient," Stone growled.

He began to walk toward his car, but half way there he turned and raised his hand to shake an admonitory finger at Jake. "This is the last time, Riley," he said. "Next time . . ."

"Mr. Stone, I've told you—you have my promise—you'll be paid your money by this day month," said Jake.

"I'd better be!"

He cranked up his car, got in, and backed away. Jake went back into the house. The two men talking had awakened the dog, who now sat up on his haunches. During the noise the car made, I drew back along the dark passageway between the buildings, and darted out behind the barn to the field's edge.

Old man Stone backed down the gravel road to the Skunk Hollow road and turned north. I was out of the range of the headlights, and I hoped Sim would find a place to hide when Stone went by. There was no sign of Sim.

He came climbing out of the ditch when I came on to the road.

"Now I suppose you found out everything," he said in a low, irritated voice. "All about how old Jake's got a million dollars in gold tied to his stepdaughter's ankle . . ."

"Oh, shut up," I said. "Jake owes old man Stone some money and he's behind paying it. He's promised to pay in a month's time—so whatever he's planning is slated to happen before then."

"If the Baker Street Irregulars hadn't done any better than this," said Sim, "Sherlock Holmes would've fired 'em."

"I know it."

"Tomorrow you can climb up and get that telescope," he said. "You owe it to both of us. Now we have to walk all the way home along the road—it's about three times as far, as I figure it."

If anything, he underestimated it. I didn't say anything. The night was fine—that was some compensation. A coolness was in the air, and the corn-smell, not so thick here along the road, was sweet. The pungence of the woods drifted down into the valley, and the sounds of the night echoed the length of Skunk Hollow—cattle lowing, dogs barking, owls hooting, and the fluting of the frogs mingling with the steady churring of crickets and katydids and the sawing rune of a pair of cicadas.

We went as fast as we could, to get out of Jake Riley's neighborhood, and we were soon up over the ridge and on that part of the road that led through the woods to the highway which curved around to Great-uncle Joe's driveway. It was safe to talk there, away from any farms.

"About those fingerprints," I said. "I've been thinking. I know just the one to give them to Mike Kurth."

"I'll bet," answered Sim in snorting doubt.

"Pete Bandheim!" I said.

"Pete!" exclaimed Sim, the moment I mentioned his old fishing pal. I could feel him grin with satisfaction. "You're right! He's just the one to do it."

8.

We Enlist Aid

Pete Bandheim was a year or two younger than Sim and I. He was the son of one of the village barbers— the one Sim and I went to—and he intended to be a barber himself. He was as sharp as a needle, and he never got caught when he got into mischief. Not many people ever suspected that he was as sharp as he was because he kept it hidden. He had the kind of face that helped. He liked to pretend he was so dumb he didn't know enough to come in out of the rain. He would let his mouth hang open a little, and get a sort of glazed look in his eyes, when he was busy talking somebody out on a limb so he could saw it off, and when he looked like that he looked as if he had rooms for rent—all the room between his ears.

He had it in for smarties. Once in a while somebody came into the barber shop when Pete was there just to sit and smart off. Then Pete would put on his dumbest face and ask questions, each one sillier than the other, until the poor fool he was baiting figured Pete didn't know beans from buckwheat. Just about the time his victim figured Pete was fair game, Pete's questions began to get sharper

and sharper, and pretty soon the smart alec was falling
with the limb Pete had sawed off. He never knew what hit
him; Pete would still be standing there looking as if he
couldn't add two and two to get four to save his life, and
his victim couldn't believe Pete had made a first-class fool
out of him.

We went around to find Pete after we had gone to
church in Sac Prairie that Sunday. We trailed him from
St. Jude's to his home and on down to the river behind
the Electric Theatre, where he was fishing for bluegills.

"Pete, we got a job for you," said Sim, the minute he
caught sight of us.

Pete shrugged. "You needed a haircut before you went
out into the country. You can wait till you get back."

"It's nothing like that," said Sim, as if he didn't know
Pete had said it only to aggravate him. "It's a ticklish
proposition. You've got to talk to Mike Kurth for us." He
paused, since Pete was paying attention only to his cork.
"Are you listening?"

"How could I do anything else?" asked Pete. "I forgot
my earplugs."

I took over. I told him about the fingerprints, and how
we needed to find out if Jake Riley's prints might be on
record somewhere. Maybe the Secret Service knew him.
Maybe he had another name. Since he was an outsider from
Chicago, it was possible that he wanted to change his name.
I explained why Mike would probably think we were playing some sort of trick on him just because we had been
right about that counterfeit nickel two months ago.

"And what do I tell him?" Pete asked.

"You'll know what to tell him," I said. "But don't mention us or Jake."

"You mean I have to make something up?"

"Sure. The end justifies the means," I said.

"That's what they said about everything from the Inquisition to the World War," he said. "You got the fingerprints?"

Sim produced them, carefully protected by glass. "Here they are," he said. "Don't mess with 'em."

"Don't intend to," said Pete.

Just then his cork plopped under and Pete pulled in a sunfish as big as Grandfather Adams' hand.

"You'd ought to have played him," chided Sim.

"You can play fish all you like," said Pete. "I'm out to catch 'em, not play 'em."

When he had his hook baited again, he held out his hand for the prints.

"Not here!" protested Sim.

"Sure, here," said Pete. "Mike Kurth is off his beat this morning. He's fishing just off Second Island. I'll take those prints right up to him."

"But he's not on duty," said Sim.

"Mike is always on duty. That's his trouble. Gimme 'em." He thrust his pole at Sim. "Here, you take this. I'll be right back."

He took the fingerprints which Sim surrendered reluctantly. Sim took his pole.

"I'll go along," I said.

"Don't let Mike see you," cautioned Sim.

Pete was already on the way. He stepped from one rock to another where they lay around the retaining wall behind the Electric Theatre until he reached the sandy shore behind the old Hahn house. Then he went up along the shore, past Elzy's house and Mr. Elky's, and plunged into the thick growth of willows along that outthrust paw of land we called "First Island." It wasn't really an island at all, though it had once been, and it was only in spring that water came down along the road embankment through Ehl's Slough and cut this land off. Now a path led up through it, among the old poplar and cottonwood trees, winding over roots and skirting little soft places where you were likely to sink into water if you walked carelessly. It smelled of the river in these woods—and of wet sand and willows, all of which made the musk that belonged to riverbottom places.

We came out to an open, sandy place, with a thin stream flowing through it, so thin that we could jump it easily. Across this sandy place, with its water-holes and its stream, was "Second Island." The near end of the island supported three giant old trees; a fourth had fallen and lay out in the water. It was a place I often came to with Father to fish for bluegills, which liked to lie under the fallen trunk.

Pete stopped. "There he is," he said.

I couldn't see anything but the top of a fishpole moving around. If it was Mike, he was fishing off the fallen tree, near the bottom of the trunk, probably leaning against all the root-mass which fanned up there where the tree had pulled out of the sandy bank when the water had washed out the earth beneath.

"I'll go ahead," said Pete.

He crossed to the tip of the island, and I went on up

along the sand to a point just behind the fallen tree. Then I cut in among the trees to where I could see.

It was Mike, all right. Mike was a tall, broad-shouldered man, with a raw, red face. He could look fierce when he was on the job, but right now he was enjoying himself. He was sitting with his back to the tree roots, with his eyes half-closed, and his hat down over his forehead to shade his face from the sun.

He heard Pete coming right away, and sat up.

I could see and hear everything where I was. Pete put on his most innocent face. Oh, that Pete! He made himself look as if his Ma had just scrubbed him clean and put clothes on him so nobody would mistake him for a hitching post. He went right up to Mike.

"Mike," he said in a husky voice, "I got to see you."

Mike looked at him with suspicion thick enough to cut. He distrusted all kids by experience.

"Mike," Pete went on, "we were got into last night."

"You mean the barber shop?" cried Mike, incredulous.

"Fact," said Pete. "I don't know how they did it, but I got their fingerprints. Thumb and forefinger. I got 'em here under glass. I want you to send 'em in and find out if they're on the records."

Mike took it as a personal insult. "Right here in my jurisdiction!" he exclaimed. "And me on the beat, too!"

He climbed excitedly out of the tree roots and jumped to the bank. "Lemme see them fingerprints," he demanded.

Pete pulled them out of his pocket. "Be careful of 'em, Mike. I took 'em off a box of powder they handled. Got 'em here under glass. It was a new box—we just unpacked it yesterday; so nobody else got to touch it."

Mike goggled at the fingerprints. "You sure done a good job!" he said. "Them doggone crooks!" He puffed himself up with indignation. "Me on the job, too! That's pure gall!" Then he got a little suspicious again. His eyes narrowed. He bent down and took Pete by the shoulder. "What'd they take?"

Pete's expression never changed. He looked so guileless you'd only have had to pin wings on to make it look as if they grew that way. He looked so dumb you'd never have thought he had enough brain cells to think up anything to tell but what he had seen.

"They took two bottles of Lucky Tiger," said Pete without blinking an eye.

"Lucky Tiger!" hollered Mike. "So maybe they was havin' trouble with their hair, hah?"

"Some people," said Pete, lowering his head and looking down with exaggerated innocence, "—some people drink it!"

Mike jumped right at that and took it. "That's it! That's it!" he hollered. "That's sure it. They went off on a toot somewheres. Oh, we'll find 'em!" Then he grew cautious once more, but it was plain that the excitement of the crime was thinning his caution. "But how'd they get in? Break in?"

Pete shook his head. "The only thing I can figure is a skeleton key."

"That's it!" agreed Mike at once. "I read about them things. I had one once." He turned and looked regretfully at his pole. "Well, I guess that finishes my fishing."

"There's no hurry," said Pete. "You just send those prints in, and we'll find out if they're known crooks. Then, if they aren't, we can always start looking for 'em. We'll have two clues."

"Two clues?" echoed Mike. "What clues besides these here fingerprints?"

Pete leaned forward and said in a loud whisper, "Two empty Lucky Tiger bottles."

"That's right!" said Mike with renewed excitement. "And they'll have fingerprints all over 'em. Oh, those fellers that think they're so smart! They don't get anything over on Mike, no sirree!"

"But right now those fingerprints are the only clues we got," said Pete. "Take good care of 'em."

"I will. I sure will. I'll take 'em over to Madison myself."

"Another thing," said Pete. "I didn't tell anybody about the robbery—not even Pa. The less is said, the more sure of themselves the crooks will be, don't you think so, Mike?"

"That's dead right," agreed Mike, admiringly. "A man'd never think it to look at you that you'd be that smart."

"So if you don't say anything and I don't say anything, maybe they'll think they didn't get found out, and they might come back for more Lucky Tiger," finished Pete.

"And I'll keep my eye on the shop every night," agreed Mike, clenching and unclenching his fingers. "And when I catch 'em. . . !" He left the dreadful carnage to Pete's imagination.

"It's a good thing we got a policeman like you in Sac Prairie!" said Pete, his voice dripping with awe and admiration.

"I enforce the laws," said Mike stoutly. "I do my duty. It's my job."

I almost burst into laughter where I stood, but I didn't dare. I backed away, keeping a big treetrunk between Mike and me, and slipped down along the sandy bank. I went back the way I had come to wait across the stream on the path on First Island for Pete to come. He came in just a minute or so.

"You can change your face now," I said. "You sure laid it on thick."

"People will believe anything," Pete said. "It depends on how you tell it." He chuckled. "I'll bet those fingerprints will be in Madison before Mike goes on duty this afternoon."

He set off in a loping run along the path, I after him.

Sim had caught two bluegills and was playing a rock bass when we got back. He was having a wonderful time. He never heard us coming, but just stood there like a professional angler playing that fish. Pete waited until he landed the bass. Sim gave the pole up reluctantly.

"Did it work?" asked Sim.

"Sure it worked," answered Pete scornfully, as if amazed that Sim could for a moment have doubted that it would. "Now get out of here so the noise don't scare the fish."

We mounted the sloping bank to Water Street, walked down it for half a block, and crossed to the harness shop. Since it was Sunday, the front door was locked. We slipped in along the north wall, along the narrow passage between the house north of the shop and the two-storey building Mr. Jones owned, and went in the back way.

Old Fred sat over his Asthmador, on the stitching-horse. He looked as if he had just come from church, with his black hat and black coat on and his Sunday suit with the gold watch-chain across his vest. He gave Sim a sharp glance.

"Been to church?" he wanted to know.

"Sure," said Sim.

"What did Reverend Zenk have to say?"

"He said that God was wonderful in his ways," said Sim promptly. "He said we had the need of some material things, and God had moved the Malakays and Mr. Schorer to write out checks."

Old Fred chuckled. "Well, that's right. You were there. We just didn't see you."

"And Ma was worried. I know," said Sim.

"You home now?" asked Fred then.

"No, we're going back," answered Sim. "Important business."

Fred laughed. "The important things are the little things," he said. "But you'll be an old man before you find it out." He looked at me. "What about you? You got important business, too?"

"Me? All I have to do is get back up to the house so we can go home to the country," I said.

Sim was anxious to go. I would just as soon have stayed in the harness shop for a while. Even though it was summer and a long time from the winter season of washing and repairing harnesses, the smell of leather and oil gave the air a kind of cool, medicinal odor. But Sim was always in a hurry to go when Fred Jones began to pour oil.

We went out the back way, down past the office, and across lots to Sim's house to pick up some cocoanut macaroons Mrs. Jones had baked the day before. I counted every one Mrs. Jones put into the cardboard box—thirty-seven!—and my mouth watered when I thought of eating these delicious "kisses," as she called them. Mrs. Jones fluttered around, birdlike.

"Couldn't you stay for dinner?" she kept asking.

I assured her we couldn't.

"How does Simoleon behave?" she asked anxiously.

"Better than I do," I said. "Sim's a good boy."

Sim kicked me as soon as his mother's back was turned.

We left the Jones house and cut through the Free-thinkers' Park, across the railroad tracks, and reached our place. Great-uncle Joe and Great-aunt Lou were waiting there for us. The whole family was there—Grandfather and Grandmother Adams, too, and nobody looking as if we were heading for the farm in a hurry. I took a look around and knew what had happened when I saw Mother busy in the pantry—she had insisted that everyone stay for dinner.

"We're staying," I said to Sim. "Long enough to eat."

He gave me a reproachful look, as if it were my fault, for we had made definite plans to go fishing in the millpond this afternoon.

"We'll still get back in time to go fishing," I said.

Grandfather cleared his throat and beckoned to me. He went out on to the back porch and sat down on the couch there. I followed him.

"Now, then," he said, "what's been going on out there?"

I knew he was wondering about Jake Riley, not about anything else. I told him everything that had happened since we had begun to spy on Jake's place.

He listened thoughtfully. Now and then he said something, more to himself than to me. Like, "Stone lends out money. Jake must have borrowed some." And, "It was foolish of you to draw attention to yourself like that at the mill. But I understand why you did it." When I had finished, he sat for a while turning over what I had said, his eyes clouded and troubled.

"What's going on, Grandpa?" I asked.

"I don't know," he said. "But it's got to do with Molly and the money that's coming to her. So much is sure. Jake promised Stone his money before another month is up— and Molly'll be eighteen in that time. Two weeks or less."

"Grandpa—there must be something more."

"I think there is, boy," he said. "Be careful. Time uncovers all things—don't you and Sim hurry time at cost to yourselves."

9.

Mr. Barton

THE next day the stranger came to the farm.

Sim and I had gone up to the oats field with Great-uncle Joe. He wanted to look over the shocks. Great-aunt Lou had been at him to start threshing, and he was looking for more excuses to put it off a little longer. Great-uncle liked to put off things, maybe because it riled her so.

Great-uncle Joe walked from shock to shock, muttering to himself that the grain wasn't ripe enough yet, when anybody could see from a hundred paces that it was just about ready to fall off if you touched a shock. Sim and I sat on the rails of the fence, watching. Neither of us saw the stranger till he was almost at the fence.

"Good morning," he said cheerily. "That your dad?" He pointed at Great-uncle Joe.

We shook our heads. "We're just visiting," I said.

He was a plainly-dressed young man, about thirty, I judged. His face was lean and thin, and had a kind of waxy complexion as if he'd creamed it. He had brown eyes, and a nose a little too long for his face, but his look was pleasant, and he smiled easily. He carried a little case with him, like a salesman. He had on a straw hat, a white shirt, a yellow tie, and a blue serge suit.

Hearing his voice, Great-uncle came hurriedly down to the fence. His heavy face shone with anticipation. Like most of the farmers around Sac Prairie, he liked to talk, especially when he was supposed to be working.

"Good morning, Mr. Stoll," said the stranger.

"Mornin'," answered Great-uncle affably. He stood expectantly waiting on his visitor to entertain him.

"My name is Barton, Mr. Stoll."

"You a salesman?"

"Well, you might call me that. The truth is, I'm making a survey." As he spoke, he opened his case and revealed some bottles of various sizes. "We're trying to find out how widely some of these products are used. Take this one, for instance." He pulled out a large bottle filled with brown liquid.

I recognized it at once. It was *Alpenkräuter;* I had to take it whenever I had a pain.

"We use that," said Great-uncle. "Sure works."

"How about this one?" asked Barton, taking out another bottle.

Great-uncle peered at it and shook his head. "No, we don't use the *Adlerika.*"

Barton went through the bottles he had in his case— just eight of them in all. Most of them were common patent medicines he was likely to find everywhere he stopped. When he finished, he closed up his case and leaned on the fence next to Great-uncle. He wasn't in any hurry to go.

"What about your neighbors?" he asked.

"Well, there's Gus Elker," said Great-uncle.

"How many people at that place?"

"Two. He's got a housekeeper now and then."

"No hired man?"

"He comes in by the day if he comes. Gus don't need him much."

"Who's on the other side?"

"Ed Burke."

"How many there?"

"Well, there's Ed and there's his wife, and their three kids and the hired man. I make it six." Great-uncle went on. "Then there's Jake Riley. Only two there, though."

"No hired man?"

"No."

"Hasn't hired anybody lately, has he?"

"Not that I know of." He turned to us. "But the boys has been over there since the last time I was there. How about it, boys?"

Sim shook his head and I said, "No hired man. Nobody. Just the two of 'em. I'd a figured you knew that," I said, looking at him hard.

"I'm a stranger to these parts," Barton said.

"Maybe you own a pair of binoculars," I said.

He smiled. "I belong to the Birdwatchers' Club of Madison," he said. "Sure. Have to have them."

"You don't go birdwatching in those shoes," I said, looking at them. "You'd slip all around."

He looked down at his shoes, then up at me.

"You need rubber soles in the woods," I said.

Sim poked me. I shut up.

Barton looked at Great-uncle. "How do I get to Gus Elker's?"

"You can follow the road here," said Great-uncle. "He lives back in the Pocket."

"Jake Riley's?"

"Oh, you have to go all the way round by the road and into Skunk Hollow, if you're driving a car," said Great-uncle. "Unless maybe you came that way?"

"Well, I didn't come through Skunk Hollow," Barton said. "I must have passed the road in."

"You come from Madison, then?" asked Great-uncle.

Barton just nodded. He looked around, sort of casual-like, and said then, "Looks like good hunting territory."

"Sure is," said Great-uncle. "I be dog if this ain't the best all-round huntin' country in the county!"

"Seen many hunters around lately?"

Great-uncle stared at him. "Not this time a year," he said, as if Barton should have known as much. "Sometimes Gus Elker and me go after fox, or Ed Burke trains his dog on coon—but that's not what a body'd call huntin'."

Barton looked around. "Mrs. Stoll says you have a hired man, Mr. Stoll. Where is he?"

"Oh, he's around somewheres."

"Hire him lately?"

"Heck, no! Burl's been with us nigh on to four years."

"Just the three of you then, and the two boys?"

"They belong to Sac Prairie."

"Yes, and we got half those bottles at our house," I said, "and that's four times too many."

Barton grinned. "Can't say I blame you. I'm just taking the survey. I don't have to sample them."

He shook Great-uncle's hand and thanked him.

"There's a real nice-speakin' feller," said Great-uncle

as he stood watching Barton walk jauntily down the lane toward the house where his car was parked.

"Sure is," I agreed. "Only I don't think his name's Barton. I don't think he's making a survey. I don't think he gives a hoot about you or anybody else on this place, now he knows Burl's been here four years."

Great-uncle Joe looked at me, mouth agape.

For a few moments nobody said anything. The sounds of the country pushed in—an indigo bunting singing not far away, grasshoppers whirring where they danced in the air, the excitement of crows along the cornfield. Then Great-uncle's face unfroze and Sim began to laugh.

"Old Timer—are you sure?" asked Great-uncle.

"That's his imagination, Mr. Stoll," said Sim. "He's got a lot of it."

"You know it's more than that," I said hotly.

"Nothing you could prove anything by," said Sim. "Except he's wearing a blue serge suit—same as that fellow in the woods that day, watching Jake Riley's house from the other side."

"If that don't beat all!" exclaimed Great-uncle, gazing after Barton as if he expected him to materialize on the spot and deny everything. Then he collected himself and said gravely, "Old Timer, I like to die if we better not set down and talk this over. You git to Gus Elker and tell him to come to the house supper time, and we'll see what we can figger out."

Gus Elker came over that night for supper, and we all sat around the table talking. Great-aunt Lou just naturally took charge of the situation, because if she hadn't, Gus and Great-uncle Joe would have spent most of the time bickering good-naturedly about every detail.

It was raining outside, and Gus had come in through it. He looked like a tramp, with his hair sticking out every which way, and his oversize clothes wet, and his expression as if the roof had fallen in. The sound of the rain closed the house in from all but an occasional bawling from the barn, where Burl Wilkins was milking the cows.

What Gus had to say was just what he had said before. He was still worrying about what his duties were as Justice of the Peace. "I'd jist as soon collar that critter," he said, "but I don't know what to charge him with. I know Jake Riley's up to somethin'."

"We all guess he is," said Great-aunt tartly. "We guessed it before, and we're still at it. We ain't practically moved a-tall, 'pears to me."

"Well, we did find out he's keeping a close watch on Molly," I put in. "And we did get some reason to believe somebody else's interested in what's going on at Riley's."

"That's so," agreed Great-uncle excitedly. He turned to Gus and told him all about Barton's visit. To hear it, you'd never have thought it was the same visit we had taken part in. Great-uncle proved that I wasn't the only one in the family with imagination—it seemed to me he had a lot more.

"Why, say, that feller called on me, too," said Gus. "Be dog if he didn'. Yestidday."

"Yesterday!" cried Great-uncle Joe. The chair on which he had been leaning back came to the floor with a thud. "An' here he was today askin' about your place an' how to git to it."

"I figgered there was something funny about that feller," said Gus, nodding gravely.

"I don't see what all that has got to do with Jake keepin' Molly penned up," said Great-aunt Lou.

"By Jukas! it all hangs together," declared Great-uncle.

"How?" asked Great-aunt flatly. "I declare to goodness, Joe, you talk before you think. You always did. You tell me where it hangs together. I'll allow it seems a mighty strange coincidence, but I don't see how it means anything that those men are coming around here just at the same time Jake's keepin' his stepdaughter close to him—locked in the house and never out of sight."

"Maybe it's got something to do with the money Jake expects to get," I said.

"The only money's comin' in is Molly's, not his'n," said Gus.

"How about the farm? Maybe he's going to sell it," suggested Sim.

"He don't own it," said Great-uncle. "It's mostly Molly's —and she won't sell."

"Maybe that's it," said Great-aunt. "That old varmint is keepin' her locked up till she signs the papers!"

Great-uncle sniffed. Clearly, he took a dim view of that solution.

Great-aunt Lou's impatience boiled over. "Heavens t' Betsy!" she cried. "There's but one thing to do, and I aim to do it. That's to go right over there and look around for myself."

"Now, Lou," said Great-uncle placatingly.

"And I'm doin' it first thing tomorrow," she finished.

Great-uncle's alarm sprang into his normally jolly face. Concern showed in Gus's face, too.

"I wouldn' do that, Mrs. Stoll, Ma'am," said Gus. "If you tumbled on to something—no tellin' what Jake Riley might do."

"Pshaw! It takes more'n the likes of Jake Riley to scare me. A woman who's lived through more'n forty years with a man like mine, never knowing what he'll do next, ain't apt to be scared by half a dozen Jake Rileys."

"Maybe if the boys go along," said Great-uncle.

"The boys can go, and welcome," said Great aunt, smiling and looking challengingly at us over her spectacles.

"Wouldn't miss it," I said.

And I wouldn't. I was itching to set foot inside that house and take a look around. At that moment I was sorry only that I didn't have my magnifying glass with me.

Later that night, lying in bed under the rain on the attic roof, Sim badgered me.

"How have you got it figured out, Sherlock?" he asked. "You're the great detective story reader. I figure you know all the answers."

I lay there thinking. Oh, it smelled good in that room with the freshness of the rain drifting in through the open windows! You felt closed away from everything and everybody, and even the owls hooting just outside sounded far away. It was a wonderful night to just lie and think; it would be a wonderful night to sleep, too.

"Turn over those gray cells," said Sim.

"Haven't *you* been thinking?" I asked. "Some things are plain as the nose on your face."

"Sure. That money Jake's expecting. It's Molly's, isn't it?"

"Has to be, as far as I can see. There's no money coming in otherwise that we know about. And his keeping her close at hand and all—that's what it adds up to."

"But how's he going to get his hands on it?"

"That's what I'd like to know. As far as I can see, nobody's coming out to give her a bag of money when she's eighteen. It's in the bank and it'll stay there till she gets it out, and I don't see her going in to get it out for him. So how?"

"I asked you."

"I know. It bothers me. It bothers me a lot. That's not all that bothers me, either. That fellow Barton."

"Ja. I knew it the minute I laid eyes on him that he wasn't what he was pretending to be," said Sim.

"You take and figure it this way," I said. "He's looking for somebody. It's not Molly. He knows where she is. He doesn't care a bit about her. He knows where Jake is. No sense looking for him. So he's looking for somebody else. But it's a funny way he goes about it. First he watches the place with binoculars . . ."

"Assuming it *was* him."

"Okeh, assuming. Maybe it wasn't. Maybe two fellows are keeping an eye on Jake Riley's place," I said. "It's still somebody else they're looking for. And they're looking as wide as the farms neighboring us—but always around Jake Riley's."

"We don't know that," Sim pointed out reasonably enough. "Somebody might be doing the same thing around Witwen or Black Hawk as here in the Mill Creek country."

"But they're looking for somebody who isn't here. They expect him to be here. That's the way I see it. And I got a kind of feeling Great-uncle Joe's right—it all hangs together somehow. And we have to find out how!"

Sim didn't say anything and I didn't say any more, just kept lying there and trying to think the puzzle out and only getting more and more mixed up trying to put together pieces that didn't seem to fit, till the soothing drumming of the rain on the roof put me to sleep.

10.

Aunt Lou Takes a Hand

GREAT-AUNT LOU did not wait even to do the dishes after dinner next day. She put on her bonnet, paying no attention to Great-uncle's indignant demands that she change her mind, and took up her umbrella, for though last night's rain had come to an end before dawn, another bank of clouds lay ominously in the southwest, black under the midday sun.

"Coming, boys?" she asked, turning to us.

We were ready, and out we went.

"Take care a my ol' woman," Great-uncle called after us.

"Hoh!" snorted Great-aunt. "Who's been takin' care of him all these years, I'd like to know!"

The day was hot and humid. Not a breath of air stirred. Last night's raindrops still clung to leaves and blades in shaded places, and the whole valley was heady with the smell of cornleaves and blossoms. The musk of the barnyard rose briefly, too, and, once we got closer to the woodlot, the pungence of the leaves. But the corn smell stood out above everything.

Not much stirred, either. Even the collie just ran along a little way, then went back to lie in a dug-out place in the shade of the barn. A few crows cawed. They were the sentinels, cawing to let the others know we were coming and telling them we didn't have guns. Everything seemed to be just lying in wait for a storm, but the cloud-bank stayed where it was; it didn't move up, it didn't settle down toward the horizon, and the sun blazed down with all the heat the sun can generate in August.

Great-aunt Lou went straight ahead without looking back or even resting. As Great-uncle Joe had said, "Ain't no turnin' that woman, once she's made up her mind." She didn't seem to mind heat or humidity; she just strode ahead, holding her umbrella like a club to beat Jake Riley with.

Up the pasture lane, past the cornfields and the woodlot, past Gus Elker's, and up over the saddle directly north of Gus's—the low place in the same ridge from the heights of which, to the west, we had turned our telescope on Jake Riley's. There was a kind of path over the saddle; you could tell it hadn't been used much lately, but at one time it had.

Great-aunt Lou marched along this path. She descended the hill and walked straight into Jake Riley's yard. Jake's dog got up and stiffened out and began to growl, but Great-aunt just pointed her umbrella at him and said, "Shut up!" and he shut.

At the foot of the porch, Great-aunt turned to us. "Mind you keep your mouths tight, boys. We're just payin' a neighborly call. I don't reckon Jake'll be any too glad to see us."

She mounted the back porch and hammered vigorously on the door with the handle of her umbrella.

Jake Riley's big voice rumbled out. "Come on in—it's unlocked."

Great-aunt opened the door and walked into the kitchen. We followed at her heels.

"Hello, Jake," she said.

The fat man was surprised. He pulled his lips back into a kind of smile, and all three chins came up at the ends with the corners of his mouth. He looked at us, one after another, and rumbled deep inside.

"You surprised me, Mrs. Stoll," he said.

"Reckon I did," replied Great-aunt. "I been over this way and figured I'd set a spell with Molly—if she's to home."

"She's home, all right," said Jake, giving Great-aunt a sharp glance. "She's home. She'll be liking to see you." He considered me carefully and said, "Ah, the fat boy!"

"I'm not fat," I said. "Just muscular."

A laugh shook his bulk. He looked back at Great-aunt. Almost reluctantly, he said, "I'll get her."

"Can't you call her, Jake?" asked Great-aunt, smiling and looking guilelessly over her spectacles. "Don't seem right to ask a man to push around all that meat for me."

Jake gazed at her and grunted. He erupted from the wicker chair in which he had been sitting, and rolled out of the room.

Great-aunt Lou's eyes flickered around. She took in the chair he had left. A slow smile grew on her lips when she saw how the chair had long ago been stretched into a shape like Jake's. Her eyes settled on the sink, where a pile of dishes stood unwashed. Then she was picking out stains on the red-checked tablecloth, and dust on the old-fashioned clock up against the wall near the stove. Her smile washed away. Her lips began to twitch.

I could tell what she was thinking. Molly Burns wasn't being given a chance to keep the house clean. Her house, too—or most of it. All but a third of it; according to law, Jake had the right to a third of his late wife's possessions, except for the money left Molly by her father. So she didn't have much freedom even in her own house.

I listened for sounds from upstairs. There wasn't anything to be heard. I listened for a key in a lock, for instance. I didn't hear anything like that. Only Jake's progress marked by the creaking of the floor overhead. Then a mutter of voices. Jake's sharp, cutting. Molly's scarcely audible.

Then they were coming down the stairs.

Jake came into the room first and headed back for his chair.

Molly was behind him. Seen up this close and by the mid-day sunlight that was in the room, Molly Burns was real pretty. A little on the slim side, with brown eyes and wavy hair, long to her shoulders. Maybe not quite as pretty as Margery Estabrook, back home. Right now she was pale, and looked tired. She was dressed in a clean, dark dress and wore faded slippers. She didn't wear any stockings, but hardly anybody did on hot days like this.

She looked at Great-aunt in a kind of bashful but hopeful way, as if she didn't want to show right out how pleased she was.

"Hello, Mrs. Stoll," she said, and smiled at Sim and me.

"Land sakes, Molly!" cried Great-aunt. "Where you been this past while? I been expectin' a visit from you, but you ain't been near the house—three, four weeks now. Ain't been feelin' poorly now, have you, Molly?"

"No, Ma'am, I'm not," answered Molly, with a quick glance at Jake.

She was afraid of him, all right. We saw it that day at the mill, and we saw it again here in her own kitchen.

"There's a lot of work," said Jake ponderously.

"You ain't lost any weight doin' it," observed Great-aunt tartly, her head cocked to one side.

Jake frowned and closed his eyes. Then he opened one again immediately, lifting away the heavy lid and regarding her with mild, half-amused irritation. "You aren't asking to help, are you, Mrs. Stoll?"

Great-aunt was momentarily taken aback.

"It's mighty nice of you," Jake went on, ignoring her flashing eyes, "because I reckon I haven't got long on this earth. No, Ma'am." His voice sank into minor key. "I've done what I promised to do. I sent down to Chicago for that coffin of mine."

"Hoh! You, Jake Riley! You been sendin' for that coffin the last two, three years," said Great-aunt derisively. "You ain't near dead yet, and by the look of you, it'll take a long time for all that to die."

"Maybe so," agreed Jake, "but I aim to get some use out of that coffin before I'm buried in it. I had it made special."

"No wonder," said Great-aunt, and laughed. "They don't make 'em big enough for that much man."

Jake remained unruffled. If he was stung, he didn't show

it. "I sent for it this morning," he went on. "I sent a telegram to Chicago. You never know when your time's coming, Mrs. Stoll. Why, you might go before me."

I got a chill out of that. He didn't exactly say it in a menacing tone, but he looked so levelly at my great-aunt, it was hardly possible to mistake his meaning.

Great-aunt Lou, however, only tossed her head. "That graveyard holler don't sound like you, Jake," she said scornfully.

"I know," agreed Jake, with mock sadness. But his gray eyes were now bright and alive with amusement. "I know I'm not well liked, but I guess it's God's will. So I'm getting my coffin and I'm keeping it right here where I can look at it all the time and be reminded that my time's coming—like everybody else's."

"That's a right noble thought, Jake," said Great-aunt. "It don't sound right, comin' from you, I declare to goodness it don't. But maybe it's a good sign. Maybe next thing we'll hear you got out at them fields of your'n. That'd be the next best sign. It's good soil to be half idle."

"Huh, huh," grunted Jake, with his eyes half-closed. "I'm not worrying about the things of this world, Mrs. Stoll—not half as much as you are."

"Well, I do declare!" cried Great-aunt sharply. "Look at who's talking!"

Molly had slipped into a chair at the table. She sat looking nervously from Great-aunt to her stepfather. Her brown eyes were shy. She was clearly afraid. She seemed to be apprehensive that the talk would take an unpleasant turn.

Jake shifted his glance from Great-aunt Lou to Molly.

He appeared to be calculating something. Then he looked squarely back to Great-aunt and broke the silence.

"Don't you be surprised, Mrs. Stoll, if you hear my Molly's getting married," he said.

A little cry escaped the girl, but it was choked back before it had full utterance. At her first sound, Jake had whipped his head around and glared at her. His expression was blank, but his eyes were hard—like that day at the mill: gray pools with flecks of ice.

"My conscience!" exclaimed Great-aunt. "And you never said a thing about it, Molly."

Molly lowered her head. You'd have thought her cheeks would be a little flushed, but she was pale—she was as white as plum blossoms. Her hands trembled, and her lower lip pushed up just as if she were about to cry.

"I haven't been figuring on it so long," she said in a low voice.

Jake Riley laughed suddenly. His voice was loud and harshly cruel. "My Molly's a quiet girl, now, Mrs. Stoll, don't you think so? To keep such a thing to herself."

"I reckon so," said Great-aunt. "I'm counting on having her over some afternoon or evening."

Silence fell. Molly looked up, a quick brightness in her eyes. Jake gazed at my Great-aunt with well-disguised shrewdness, as if he wanted to find any clue to her intentions.

"After all," Great-aunt went on, "we'll all have to do what we can for the time of her wedding."

Jake shifted in his chair. "Maybe I could come over, too. I ain't seen Joe for a spell."

"Maybe," said Great-aunt. "That is, if Molly's agreeable?"

Jake just turned his head a little in Molly's direction. He never said a word. He didn't need to. She took the hint.

"I sure am, Mrs. Stoll," said Molly with almost pathetic eagerness.

Great-aunt nodded as if that were settled. She said, "I'll be letting you know, Molly."

Jake grunted again. He closed his eyes and opened one again, fixing Great-aunt with it. "Might be my nephew from Chicago could come, too. If he's here. I'm expecting him."

Great-aunt sniffed. "If he minds his manners," she said tartly. "Is he behaving now? I mind how he was mixed up in bootlegging and those gangs down in Chicago."

"My nephew George?" cried Jake, his whole face registering indignation.

"George Riley. Your nephew," said Great-aunt Lou flatly. "To tell the truth, I thought he was in jail, but he must be out again—most likely on parole."

"Mrs. Stoll, you shouldn't joke so before these innocent boys," said Jake, looking at us for the first time.

I tried to look innocent. Sim never had to try. He always looked as if life had just gone around him.

"Especially," Jake went on, "about the man Molly might marry."

Great-aunt almost gave herself away, she was that shocked. She just said, "I surely wouldn't say a word against any man Molly wants to marry."

Jake Riley began to laugh. The vast pile of him trembled and shook with mirth. There was something hard and unconvincing about his laughter. It was something that seemed to exist apart from the unsmiling mouth and the hard gray eyes.

Great-aunt Lou stood up suddenly. She was flustered and had a hard time keeping from showing it.

"I'll say good-night now," she said. And to Molly she added, "I'll telephone you some night, Molly—and you and Jake come right over."

She could hardly wait until we were out of hearing before she burst out. "Short and sweet," she said in an angry voice. "That girl's being held," she went on, chopping off her words. "Ain't no two ways about it. You seen them dishes, and that dust, and that tablecloth. Molly's a clean girl." She shook her head decisively. "That girl's not getting married unless she's set on it. Not till I hear it from her own lips when that wicked man's nowhere in sight!"

"That's how he's planning to get hold of Molly's money," I said. "By marrying her to his nephew."

"We'll see about that," said Great-aunt.

"But what can you do?" I asked.

She hesitated a long time before she replied. Then she said, "When the time comes, we'll think of something."

So she did not know any more than I did. Or Sim. I looked back at Sim. We were walking single file in the path, Great-aunt Lou in the lead, and hurrying, because the cloud-bank in the southwest had pushed up over the sun and its great dark shadow had brought dusk to the woods where we walked. Sim's face didn't give anything away. He was just thinking; he never even saw me turn around. He was looking straight ahead of him and walking more by intuition than anything else.

When we came to the house, Great-uncle Joe got only slight satisfaction in response to his questions.

"That ornery old man is fixin' to marry Molly off to his nephew," cried Great-aunt Lou, her voice betraying her vexation at her helplessness to put an end to Jake Riley's plans without delay.

"Not George!" said Great-uncle, incredulous.

"George," said Great-aunt with finality.

"I like to die if I can believe that," said Great-uncle, sitting down heavily on the edge of the porch.

"I heard him with my own ears," said Great-aunt. "The boys, too."

Great-uncle looked to us. I nodded. Sim was still thinking; he had that faintly pained expression on his face that indicated that wheels were going around between his ears.

"You know how Jake Riley likes to joke," said Great-uncle. "He was leadin' you up the garden path."

"Jake Riley ain't leadin' me nowheres," said Great-aunt. "But I took it from what he said it was so. Anyways, Molly was right there—she didn't deny she was gettin' married."

"Did she say it was to George?"

"No, not in so many words. But she didn't say she wasn't, either. Just sat there."

"Hoh!" snorted Great-uncle. "Trust a woman every time to jump to the worst conclusions. I don't figger it out that way a-tall. Maybe she's gettin' married—and it's Jake who's keepin' her back. That's more like the way it is, to my way a thinkin'."

Great-aunt Lou just looked at him. That look was enough. It should have withered him or at least shrunk five pounds off him. Then she stalked into the house.

He followed her with an injured glance. Then he turned to us.

"How'd it look to you, Old Timer?" he asked.

"It looks bad," I said. "Jake Riley's sent for his coffin."

"Oh, that coffin!" Great-uncle burst out laughing. "That does it! Jake's been talkin' that way as long as I known him. Sendin' for his coffin!"

"This time he really did it," I said. "He sent a telegram."

Great-uncle got to his feet and started for the kitchen door. "I'll jest rile up my ol' woman a little. That coffin! That's one a Jake's oldest jokes! Always jars the women-folks."

When the screendoor slammed behind him, I turned to Sim. "What's going on behind your face?"

"I figure I know who it is those strangers are looking for," he said. "Assuming you were right when you said they weren't interested in Jake or Molly, but in somebody else."

"Okeh, Watson," I said. "Who?"

"George," said Sim.

"That's assuming everything Jake Riley said is so."

"Let's assume it is," he said. "You let your Great-uncle assume what he likes. We'll go the other way."

11.

Pete Reports

We were almost at the edge of the woods beyond the pasture east of the house, on the way to the millpond to fish, when Great-aunt Lou's call echoed through the valley.

"Steve! You, boy!"

"You gonna answer that?" asked Sim darkly.

"She knows we're going fishing," I said. "She wouldn't have called unless something important came up."

Sim threw his pole down. He sat down beside it. "All right," he said. "You go. I'll wait here."

I left my gear with him and ran down the pasture and along the lane toward the house. Great-aunt Lou stood on the back porch. She eyed me severely over her spectacles.

"Land sakes! A body could holler her lungs out. I didn't hear you answer. If I hadn't a seen you, I'd never known you were comin'," she said.

"What is it, Auntie?"

"It's the telephone. Says it's important."

"It's Ma," I said. "I'll have to go home."

"It ain't your Ma," said Great-aunt Lou.

I went in to the telephone, picked up the receiver, and said "Hello?"

"It's Pete. Got a report on those fingerprints."

"What is it?"

"I better not say over the telephone. You come in."

"Did you find out anything at all?" I wanted to know.

"You'll be surprised," he said, and rung off.

I stood there a minute. What to do? I knew Sim had his heart set on going fishing. I couldn't run back there and say we were going into Sac Prairie again. He'd just blow up. I turned around. Great-aunt Lou watched me suspiciously, her eyes narrowed, her lips pursed.

"Auntie, don't look for us back for dinner," I said. "We may get a chance to ride into town."

"You'll be back for supper?"

"Oh, sure."

I ran back to where Sim waited. By the time I got to him, I had things pretty well figured out. I just picked up my pole and the rest of the gear and started out again.

Up the rest of the pasture, under the fence, and into the woods. I knew it would be only a matter of time before Sim's curiosity got the best of him. Just about the time we got to the Skunk Hollow road where it wound through the woods west of the ridge which ended in the Mill Bluff, he opened up.

"What was all that about?" he asked.

"Pete," I said. "He got a report on those fingerprints of Jake's."

"He did! What'd he get?"

"Didn't say. Said we'd have to come into town to find out."

We crossed the road and plunged into the woods on the other side. We had to get through Ed Burke's fence, then follow up the ridge to the saddle west of the Mill Bluff, from which we could go down along a winding road on the side of the bluff to the millpond.

"Well, aren't we going?" demanded Sim.

"How can we?" I asked. "You want to go fishing. I know how crazy you are for fishing. We've had to put it off so much already. The Mill Creek Irregulars' business will have to wait."

Sim sighed the same way he did when he was dealing with some balky farmers in the harness shop. It was his best what-I-don't-all-have-to-put-up-with sigh. "Good Gosh!" he cried. "We can always go fishing."

"Oh, *I* know that," I said. "I didn't think *you* knew it."

"Sometimes I think, like your Ma says, you're not all there," he said. "Here we are in the middle of the woods and no way to get to town!"

"Oh, I don't know," I said. "We're just about at the millpond. This is Wednesday morning and there'll be a lot of business at the mill and the store. I figure we can always hitch a ride into town from there. That is, if you think we should go."

"If I think we should go!" he said in disgust. "After I went to all the trouble to get those fingerprints!"

He kept at me all the way over the saddle and down the north face of the Mill Bluff. It was a lucky thing I was ahead of him, or he'd have seen the grin on my face. He wouldn't have liked that. We went down the road to the side of the hill facing the pond. The muted hum of the mill drifted across the water, and from our right came the

rushing of the falls. I sort of hesitated, so as to give him
the lead if he wanted it.

Sim brushed past me, heading for the narrow walk just
above the falls. He started right off across the walk, heading for the birch and willows and maples which shored up
the rough stone wall of the dam on the other side of the
falls.

"Going to fish on Grell's side?" I shouted above the noise
of the falls.

He turned when he got to the far side, halting me on the
narrow plank walk. "You can fish if you want to," he said.
"I'm going into town if I can hitch a ride."

"Well, I'll go along," I said. "We can always fish."

We went on around the east bank of the pond, past the
Grell house where it stood among the trees, past the old
fishing-holes where I used to fish with Grandfather Adams
and Grandfather Grendon, straight on to the mill.

"We can leave our stuff at the mill," said Sim.

I nodded and pointed. "And there's our ride," I said.

Up past the store, along the edge of the pond, stood an
ice-house. Every winter old Sam, the iceman, came out
with a crew and cut big blocks of ice out of the millpond,
away from where the skaters used the pond. He stored
them in the ice-house, in sawdust, and all summer long he
had ice to take around to the houses in Sac Prairie. Old
Sam had just finished loading ice and was coming down the
road from the ice-house on his way back to town. There
was plenty of room on the wagon-seat for both of us, and
when we waved him down, he just motioned us to climb on.

Pete was sweeping up the barber shop when we got there.

Mr. Bandheim was just finishing up a haircut. Sim would have rushed right in, but I held him back.

"We'll sit down on the bench outside," I said. "Remember, Mr. Bandheim doesn't know anything about it."

We sat down. Mr. Bandheim gave us a mighty curious look. Most of the occupants of the bench in front of the barber shop were old-timers who came down town to soak up the sun and talk about the days gone by and how much better things were then than they were now. Mr. Bandheim was a short, wiry man. His movements were quick and expert. He was a quiet one; he never said much, but he knew what was going on.

When he finished the haircut and the customer had come out, Mr. Bandheim came out, too, to go next door for a cup of coffee. When he went past us, he said, "Whatever you boys are up to—don't get caught!" and grinned.

As soon as he was out of sight, we went into the shop.

"What'd you find out?" demanded Sim.

Pete put on his dumbest expression. "About what?" he asked.

"You know, you know—the fingerprints!" cried Sim, exasperated.

"Listen," said Pete in his most aggravating manner, "*I* didn't find out anything. It's all hearsay. I got it from Mike. He came in here early this morning . . ." He stopped suddenly and glanced meaningfully past us.

We turned. There was Mike Kurth, all dressed up in his uniform, peering suspiciously into the barber shop, his face all but pressed to the glass. Pete waved to him.

"This is all your fault," Pete went on, accusingly.

"Mike's haunting the place. He's expecting to make an arrest any minute."

"The fingerprints," I reminded him.

"Give me time," said Pete. "You're always in a hurry. Well, Mike came in here early this morning, and he showed me the report he got. The fingerprints are on file, all right—in Chicago. They belong to Jacob Ancel Riley."

"We know that," said Sim impatiently. "We told you that."

"The said Riley," Pete went on, "once served a little time for larceny. In Illinois. He got out about ten years ago."

"How much time?" asked Sim practically.

"Seven years."

"Well," said Sim appreciatively, "it must have been grand larceny!"

"They had his fingerprints, and so far Mike hasn't got any further than to figure out there's no Jacob Ancel Riley—no Riley, at all—in his jurisdiction. He hasn't thought about Jake Riley out in Skunk Hollow yet. And I hope he doesn't think of him, either." He paused once more and waved again at the window.

Mike Kurth was going by a second time, pretending not to be looking in, but with his eyes rolled to their corners peering into the barber shop as if he expected a robber to come out of the back room with his arms full of Lucky Tiger bottles.

"Because, if he does," Pete went on, "the way we framed him, he'll put handcuffs on Jake the minute Jake sets foot inside the village limits."

That gave me a momentary twinge, but I rallied. "Don't

worry about that," I said. "Jake's not traveling any farther than the store at the mill, and it's not often he goes farther'n his back yard."

"Mike didn't give you the report," said Sim.

Pete laughed. "He's carrying it around as if it was made of gold. I just barely had time enough to read it."

The more I thought about how impetuous Mike Kurth was, the less I liked it. He was entirely likely to think about Jake Riley and go tearing out to Skunk Hollow with a warrant for his arrest.

"You'd better call Mike off," I said to Pete.

"*I'd* better!" he hollered. "Who started this thing, any-way?"

"Well, it was your story," I said.

"Let him stew," Sim said. "Mike won't do any damage."

"Like fun he won't!" I said. "Look—maybe he'll talk to Pete's dad. Then what? Maybe we shouldn't have told him that tale in the first place."

"If we hadn't, he wouldn't have sent in the prints," Pete pointed out.

Sim thought all this over and began to nod his head. "That's right," he said. "But he'll have to be told some-thing else now." He was beginning to worry. I never knew whether Sim was more afraid of breaking the law than of just the law. "You'll have to tell him something, Pete."

Just then Mike showed up again. Pete beckoned fran-tically to him.

"I'll tell him the truth," he said with a poker face. "If he pinches you boys, I can't help it."

I wasn't worried, but Sim just froze.

Mike came in, looking from one to the other of us as if he were trying to decide which one had the goods.

In the little time it took Mike to get into the barber shop, Pete's face had undergone one of those lightning changes. He stood there looking as if he didn't know the difference between up and down.

"Mike," he said in a voice that was scarcely more than a husky whisper, "I made a terrible mistake."

Mike stared at him as if hypnotized. He didn't say a word.

"Those bottles of Lucky Tiger—they weren't stolen at all!"

"What?" roared Mike.

Pete never flinched. He stood his ground, shaking his head. "I found out Pa sold 'em," he said.

For a moment Mike stood unmoving. Then he let out a great sigh. "Well, you didn't get broke' in at all," he said. But the grin that was forming on his red face vanished suddenly. "The fingerprints!" he said, raising his voice. "You got them fingerprints of that crook Riley. Larceny, they said. Seven years." His eyes lit up. "I know!" he bellowed. "He's been here—threatening you, ain't he? That's it!"

It was an effort even for Pete to keep on wearing that innocent-looking face. "No, it's not like that at all, Mike," he said. "I figure he must have dropped in here for a haircut. Passing through town. And he maybe picked up that box of powder."

Mike groaned. "Passing through!" he repeated. "Another crook slipped through my fingers!" Then he grew suspicious again. "But what would he be wantin' to pick up a box of powder for?" he demanded.

"He liked the smell of it," said Pete.

He stepped over to the shelf which ran beneath the long mirror across the south wall, snatched up a box of talcum powder, and waved it in front of Mike's nose. A cloud of sweet-smelling powder mushroomed out. Mike coughed and sneezed.

"It does smell nice," he agreed.

"Here comes Pa," said Pete abruptly. "Remember, Mike, we don't say a word."

Mike retreated hastily, as if he were still a silent partner in a full-fledged conspiracy to trap a dangerous criminal. He went out as Mr. Bandheim came in, and we started edging out, too. Mr. Bandheim just looked at us and whistled.

"I sure didn't think I was gone long enough for you almost to get yourselves caught," he said. "Mike must be getting soft."

Pete winked and grinned.

"You got us wrong, Mr. Bandheim," I said. "We're not crooks—we're detectives."

He laughed. "I know kids," he said. "I was a kid not too long ago myself. And my Dad never got over being a kid. Get along with you," he finished, as a customer came into the shop.

"What now?" asked Sim, once we were back on Water Street. "How do we get out to the farm again?"

"We can always hitch a ride," I said. "But I'm for asking Grandpa Adams to take us out."

"I vote for your Grandpa," said Sim.

We headed for home, across lots.

Grandfather Adams was sitting in the garden picking beans. He saw us before we saw him. He was laughing when we came up.

"Can't keep away?" he said. "Now, I like Sac Prairie, but I didn't think it'd have much appeal for a growing boy."

"We had business in town," I said. "Grandpa, will you get out the car and take us back to Uncle Joe's?"

He stood up. "What's going on?"

I told him about the fingerprints and Pete's story and Mike Kurth.

He laughed so hard he had to hold his sides. "Oh, Great God in Heaven!" he cried. "That boy," he said, when he had sobered up, "that boy comes by it naturally. His Grandfather Bandheim was a practical joker all his life. Why, I recollect the time he got up in the night and moved all the stakes the railroad company had laid out—made it look as if the right-of-way was going straight through some of the best houses and barns in town! They had such an uproar they got together a town meeting to protest before they found out the railroad company never put down those stakes!

"And another time, when he had an ornery neighbor who didn't want him fishing or swimming in his pond—there weren't any fish in it, anyway—old man Bandheim caught himself a whopping string of fish in the river, then came back and sat fishing in Breunig's pond till Breunig caught him and chased him off. Then he just pulled up his string of fish and went home. All the rest of that day and half the night, Breunig was fishing in his pond trying to catch fish like those Bandheim had and old man Bandheim laughed himself sick telling the story for years after. It wasn't any-

thing for him, either, to get up in the night with a cowbell
and go into Breunig's cornfield and ring that bell till Breunig got up and chased that bell clear through his field trying to catch the cattle he thought had got into his corn!
Yes, boy, Pete comes by it naturally."

Hearing all the racket, Mother came out on the back
porch. "For Heaven's sake!" she cried. "Are you boys back
in town again?"

"Ma, we had a little business in town," I said. "Now
Grandpa's going to take us out."

"Business," scoffed Mother. "What business have you
got to do, I'd like to know?"

Grandfather Adams picked up the kettle of beans he had
gathered. "Never underestimate a boy's business matters,
Rose," he said. "All things are relative." He thrust the
beans at me. "Here, boy, take them to your mother."

"Grandpa," I said, "we have to get back there. We have
to keep an eye on such a dangerous criminal."

Grandfather just grinned. "I'll get the car out of the
garage," he said.

I took the beans into the house.

My sister stopped practicing the piano and came out into
the kitchen. "Why don't you just move in here and be done
with it?" she asked, snickering.

Before I could give her the answer she deserved, Mother
said, "Have you boys had dinner?"

I could have got out of it, but Sim couldn't. The thought
of food overpowered him.

"No, Mrs. Grendon, we haven't," he said. "And I don't
think we'll get back to Stoll's in time for it."

"Then you boys can't go until you've had dinner," said Mother. "That's all there is to it."

I could have kicked Sim. I wanted to get back out to the Mill Creek country fast. There was no telling what larcenies Jake Riley might be up to.

12.

We Meet Mr. Morton

AFTER dinner, Grandfather Adams put us both into the front seat beside him, and started out along the nearest street to the Lower Mill Road and the country to which it led.

"I don't know what you're so anxious about, boy," he said to me. "As far as I can see, Jake isn't running away."

"He served time for larceny," I said. "He's keeping Molly prisoner. No telling what he's planning now."

"Well, now, aren't you jumping to conclusions?" asked Grandfather quietly. "Just because a man makes one mistake is no sign he's going to make another. Seems to me the trouble with the world today is just that attitude of yours —lack of charity."

"Seven years' worth is a lot of larceny," I said.

"Don't be too hasty to judge people," he answered, "I'll grant you, I think Jake Riley's a wicked man, but he may have reformed some since he got out of jail. And that's a mistake he's paid for. Seven years is a long time to be locked up. How'd you like to be kept away from your funnypaper collection and your favorite fishing places and all that food you stow away for seven years?"

The thought sent a chill down to the bottom of my feet. "I intend to keep the law," I said.

"Don't you figure most people do?" he asked.

"I guess so."

"Or else we'd never have enough jails," said Grandfather. "Now what are you boys planning?"

"Grandpa," I said, "I don't think we ought to tell you. We're operating as the Mill Creek Irregulars, and we'd have to take a vote on it."

"That's right," agreed Sim.

Grandfather Adams chuckled.

"We could make him an honorary member," suggested Sim then.

"I'd like that," said Grandfather. "Being honorary member, I wouldn't have to pay dues."

"All right, then," I said, "you're a Mill Creek Irregular. And what we have to do is separate Jake Riley from Molly Burns long enough to get her away from him so she don't have to marry his nephew."

"Hold on!" cried Grandfather. "You're way ahead of me. What's this about Jake's nephew?"

I told him.

For a while Grandfather Adams didn't say anything. He just kept on driving. I could tell he was thinking. He was looking straight ahead, watching the road, but he wasn't thinking about the road.

"I don't like the sound of that," he said presently. "If Jake has any such plans, it's plain it's to get his hands on Molly's money . . ."

"Larceny," I said.

He nodded. "And separating him from her at this point might be very ticklish—*very* ticklish. I hope you boys know what you're doing."

"We're all in it," I said. "Auntie made up her mind, and that about settles it."

"Just remember, we have telephones," he said. "In case you need help or anything goes wrong. Separating them isn't going to be enough—it's keeping them separated. Besides, you may be acting on a whole set of mistaken assumptions. Molly may not want to be taken away. What does Louisa think?"

"She thinks Molly'll be glad to get away," I said.

He turned this over in his mind and finally nodded. "Just the same, if Gus Elker or your Great-uncle get to taking out their guns for anything but a fox hunt, boy, you head for cover."

"Grandpa," I said, "just about anything is safe from Uncle Joe and Gus Elker, even with guns. Once or twice they got foxes, but I don't know yet that those times weren't accidents."

Grandfather laughed heartily. Then he sobered up, just as we drove toward the mill. "Only remember," he said, "you're able to make decisions on your own. Make wise decisions. The entire hope of education is to prepare men to make wise decisions. Don't disappoint me."

"I won't," I promised. "Grandpa, you'll have to leave us off at the mill. Our poles are there."

He stopped the car and looked at me, waiting for an explanation.

I told him how we had started from the mill. "Now," I finished, "Sim'll want to fish."

Grandfather Adams drove on. He was grinning and there was a glint in his eye. He was relaxed and drove along the winding road through the lush August countryside as if he enjoyed it. I was willing to bet he heard and could name every bird that called, and he probably saw every painted turtle that sunned itself on the bank of the creek.

He drew up at the mill. "If you're going to fish," he said, "I'll just drive on and have a talk with Louisa."

Sim stirred to life. "We can always fish," he said.

"I figured to let you fish," I said, "and I'll go up on the ridge and have another look at Jake Riley's place."

"Not without me," said Sim.

I ran in and got our paraphernalia, thanking Mr. Lodde for letting us keep it there.

"Fish're biting today," he said. "Good."

"We'll be back," I said.

I went out to the car and put the poles in the back.

"Fish are biting good today," I said. "Mr. Lodde told me."

Sim growled, "We can always fish."

"Just remember you said it," I said.

Grandfather said nothing. He backed the car around and took off for the farm.

He delivered us in a few minutes from the mill. It was not yet two o'clock, and I headed straight for the telescope while Sim put the poles and bait away. Grandfather got out of the car and went into the house to talk with Great-aunt Lou.

When I came down with the telescope he glanced at me

and said, "Remember, now, an ounce of prevention is worth a pound of cure. Don't do anything reckless."

"No, Grandpa," I said. "But just the other day you told me nothing ventured, nothing gained."

Grandfather grinned. "Sometimes I don't know whether that boy's sharp or just a smart alec," he said to Great-aunt Lou.

I went out. Sim was waiting impatiently. For a boy who had started to go fishing, he had changed quite a lot since morning.

"I don't know what we'll see," I said, "but it's a sure thing we'd better keep an eye on that place."

Sim started out walking. He paid no attention to deer-flies or the heat. When Sim walked fast, it was all I could do to keep up with him.

I was winded when we got to the top of the ridge. I handed the telescope to Sim.

"You set it up," I said. "I'm bushed."

Sim took the telescope out of the case and put it to-gether.

I sat down with my back to a tree behind Sim. Here on the top of the ridge a breeze blew fitfully. The deerflies didn't try to prevail against it. It was fresh and sweet with the smell of the woods and the cloying musk of black-berries. Overhead, the leaves made a hushing sound.

"See anything?" I asked after a while.

"Nah," said Sim.

"Jake in sight?"

"Sitting on his porch reading a newspaper."

Sim rolled back from the telescope and lay there with

his hands clasped under his head, looking up through the trees to the sunlit sky.

"You can't see anything up there," I said.

"I was just thinking," he said. "What can we hope to find out doing this? We know he's keeping Molly all but locked up. She's not getting out of his sight. We know why. What can we find out by watching here?"

"You're running on one cylinder," I said. "We're waiting for sight of George, that's what. The way I figure it, we'll more or less have to keep an eye on Jake's place from now on. We can't do it alone. Gus and Great-uncle Joe'll have to help."

Sim wasn't listening much to what I was saying. He had raised up on one elbow and lay there with his head cocked to one side. He was listening to something, but not to me.

"What's the matter?" I asked.

"Listen," he said quietly.

I listened. Jake's dog, which had been barking, was still. Off to the west along the ridge, crows cawed. Two blue jays scolded somewhere. A chipmunk chattered angrily.

I put all the sounds together and came up with the answer. "Somebody else's in the woods."

"Sounds like it," he agreed. "But where?"

I listened a while. The jays and the chipmunk seemed to be calling northwest of us.

"Over there," I pointed. "Somebody on the ridge west of Riley's."

Sim turned again to the telescope and shifted it to bear down on the ridge. The chipmunk's scolding died away, and the blue jays' *thief, thief* drifted northward with the birds.

"Don't see a thing," said Sim presently, and sat up.

"Let me look."

I stretched out at the telescope and looked over the ridge all along its length, foot by foot. There was nobody in sight. The woods were empty of anything but one raccoon that was making its way through the underbrush near a stand of blackberry canes.

A blue jay cried out again, nearer to us. And at the same time a crow flying in from the north to cross the ridge just west of us gave out with his alarm caw. Then all was silence again.

"Jake still on the porch?" asked Sim.

I turned the telescope back toward Jake Riley's place. There he sat, just as if he had never moved.

"Still there," I said. "And no sign of Molly."

"He's probably got her locked up again," said Sim.

I moved back and turned around. I was going to say something to Sim about planning our time in such a way that both of us wouldn't be tied down to watching Jake Riley's place, but the words never came out.

About ten feet behind Sim, a man stood against a tree. He wasn't anyone I had ever seen before. He wore a dark green shirt, brown pants, and tennis shoes.

"Well, boys," he said, seeing I had seen him, "stargazing?"

Sim sort of shriveled. He darted a quick glance over his shoulder. When he saw it wasn't a monster standing there, he relaxed a little.

"No," I said.

He came forward. He moved like a cat. I could see why he had worn tennis shoes into the woods. It wasn't the smartest thing to do, all things considered—like briars and brambles and snakes—but tennis shoes would help you move pretty quietly.

There wasn't any point in trying to lie to him. He had been standing there long enough to know what I was looking at. "We were watching Jake Riley's house," I said.

His little brown eyes seemed to smile when he grinned. "What for?"

"We were looking to catch sight of Molly," I said.

He gave me a speculative look. What I had said was true enough. He seemed to be weighing it. "That's the girl with him? His stepdaughter?"

I nodded. Sim never said a word. He just sat there looking and listening. I could see he was nervous.

"Who're you?" I asked.

"My name's Morton," he said. "I'm just hiking through."

His name might have been Morton, but it was a cinch he wasn't hiking through. He wouldn't be hiking in these woods. Over the hills east of Sac Prairie, yes. On the Mill Bluff, perhaps. At the Ferry Bluff and along the river there, very likely. But not here behind the Fair Valley Store, not here in the middle of nowhere, so far from any road. He wasn't just hiking.

He came up then, dropped to his knees, and looked through the telescope.

"Hm," he said. "Pretty good view you got from here."

"And the sun don't reflect from our glass either," I said.

He gave me a sharp look. He touched the telescope. "Yours?" he asked.

"Grandpa's," I said.

"He a star-gazer, too?"

"Only at night," I said.

He grinned again. He wasn't exactly unfriendly. He gestured toward Jake Riley's house. "You don't estimate that a rifle bullet might find its way up here?"

"It might," I said. "But it'd land up in the tree somewhere—not here on the ground. We're back of the trees." I shut up when I felt Sim's foot pressing against mine. I was talking too much. "But why should we expect a rifle bullet?" I asked.

"Boy Scouts should be alert," he said.

"Sim's a Lone Scout," I said. "I'm nothing. What's that got to do with it?"

He didn't answer. Instead he asked, "What'd Riley want to lock up his stepdaughter for?"

"Maybe she's got a beau," I said. "She wants to run away. Get married. Jake wouldn't want that. Jake might have other plans for her. So he keeps her where he can watch her."

His face wore a wide-eyed expression. "Is that so?" he asked. "Who would her beau be?"

"Mister," I said, "don't ask me to violate a confidence."

He chuckled. "So you're watching for Molly. And what do you plan to do?"

"Why, we'll help her escape—if she wants to escape."

He got up. He looked down at me and then at Sim and back to me. "Well, good luck!" he said. "I hope you help her get away. Maybe you can be best man at her wedding."

"Not me," I said. "The only thing I like about weddings is the food."

"You look it," he said.

Then he walked away. He hardly made a sound. He went west along the ridge. Sim waited until he was out of sight; then he wanted to say something. I shook my head.

We sat listening. We couldn't hear him, of course. But in a little while a jay called. Then two chipmunks scolded, their whistling cries shrill in the warm afternoon. Then another blue jay, followed by the rattling irritation of a red squirrel, chattering. The direction was west, then northwest.

"That makes two of 'em," I said. "First Barton—now this one. You notice how he said he was just hiking through —and he knew her name was Molly and that she was Jake's stepdaughter. He knows all about Jake."

"The minute he was satisfied we were looking for Molly, he beat it," observed Sim. "Don't that make you think?"

"It sure does. They don't give a hoot about Molly. What I think is this—you and I have got a hold on the wrong end of this case," I said.

"That's what I figure," said Sim. He got up and picked up the telescope. "We're wasting our time here."

"Why?" I was loath to give up the post.

"Because they're watching that house like eagles, that's why. Nobody could get in or out there without their knowing it. So what're we doing?"

What he said made sense. He put the telescope back into the case. I took it to carry it home.

"Fine Irregulars we are," I said. "If we were over in London, Sherlock Holmes would have fired us a week ago."

"Well, you're the great detective," said Sim sarcastically. "What do we do next?"

"I'll tell you," I said. "Ten to one that fellow Morton's

got a car parked on the Witwen road. That being so, we can turn the tables on him. We'll get his license. We'll call it in to Grandpa Adams, and he can check it with the license bureau in Madison. That way we'll find out his name."

"By the time we get over there, he'll be gone," said Sim.

"Not the way Uncle Joe drives."

We hurried back to the house as fast as we could.

Great-uncle Joe took us around through Skunk Hollow and over to the Witwen road. There was a car there, all right. It was a Ford sedan. It was parked in at the peaviner right next to the square pile of smelly peavines.

We took the license down as we passed by, and the moment we got back to the house, we telephoned it in to Grandfather Adams.

About forty minutes later, Grandfather called back.

The license belonged to a Rent-a-Car Agency in Madison.

13.

A Plan to Rescue Molly

THAT evening at the supper table, Great-aunt Lou took over.

"It's time we set down and talked about Jake," she said. "I sent for Gus."

Great-uncle Joe looked warily at her. "Now, Lou—don't you go gettin' any idees about meddlin' with Jake."

"Hoh! If a body waited for you and Gus to do anything, that wicked old man would have Molly married off before you lifted a finger. If 'twas chasin' down some poor fox with a gun, wouldn't be any holdin' you."

Great-uncle raised his eyes heavenward. "Old Timer," he said, "I don't know how a man a my parts got mixed up with a woman. I don't for a fact."

Great-aunt Lou just smiled. It was plain to see that she had heard this before.

"I don't know but what every time you mix into something, Lou, things happen that ain't planned," said Great-uncle.

Great-aunt looked at us and said, "My old man bucks and kicks like a horse new to harness."

"If it comes right down to it," said Great-uncle, " 'tain't our business."

"We're neighbors, ain't we?" demanded Great-aunt Lou, her eyes flashing behind her spectacles. "You don't sit here if Ed Burke's granary catches fire, do you?"

"That's different."

"How so? I declare to goodness I don't see the difference. If Ed's granary is afire, we all help to put it out. If somebody broke in and robbed Molly's place, we'd all try to catch him. Just because it's her stepfather tryin' to take her money shouldn't make any difference—it's a kind of robbery, just the same. And we don't have to catch anybody—we only have to separate the two of 'em long enough so's Molly don't have to marry a man she don't want to."

Sim looked at me with a meaningful glance. He knew as well as I did that whether Molly got married or not was probably not as important as whatever else was going on. We were still working away at the wrong end of the stick and we both knew that if we weren't careful the Mill Creek Irregulars were going to fail their first case. But there wasn't any other end within sight to take hold of.

Great-uncle Joe couldn't answer Great-aunt's logic. What she said held together. It made sense. Even he saw it. He frowned darkly and looked unhappy.

"Just the same," Great-aunt Lou went on, "I'm not sure I'll be wanting help. Like as not you and Gus would botch everything up."

"Hoh!" snorted Great-uncle scornfully. But in the next moment, his heavy face wrinkled cautiously. "Now, Lou, that Jake Riley is dangerous to get tangled with. Molly has

got to be took care of. Sure, that's so. But I wouldn'
trust Jake Riley. He's as like as not to use his gun—and he
won't care if he's aimin' it at you."

Outside, the dog began to bark. Great-uncle's dog had all
kinds of barks. This one was the company bark, which
meant someone was coming, but, since the bark was not
urgent, it was someone the dog knew.

Gus Elker came up the back porch steps and stood at the
screendoor, peering into the kitchen. "Evenin', all," he said.

"Come in, Gus," cried Great-uncle. "My ol' woman is
fixin' to git Molly away from Jake."

Gus came in apologetically. "That's the right thing,
Ma'am," he said. "On'y—it's got to be done legal."

He pulled out a chair and sat down, and for a long minute nobody said anything. From outside came the sound of
Burl Wilkins' shouting at the cows, and one of the pigs
squealing, and crows cawing overhead. Then Gus shifted
around and turned his melancholy eyes on my Great-aunt.

"Legal," he said again, with emphasis. "I like to know
what you're figgerin' on, Ma'am."

"Well, the first thing is to get her and Jake down here
some time," she answered. "Ain't no use invitin' her alone,
because Jake won't let her come. So he'll have to be invited,
too. Then we'll separate them and get her out of the country for a spell—long enough till her birthday's past and the
money's come to her. She bein' of age then, Jake can't do
nothing."

Great-uncle cleared his throat. "That's all easier said
than done."

"Is it legal?" asked Gus. "Seein' as how I'm Justice a the
Peace, I have to be sure it's legal."

"If Molly's agreeable, it's legal enough," answered Great-aunt tartly.

"Even sayin' we could separate 'em," Great-uncle went on in his slow way, leaning on the table, "how we gonna snake her away? Can't use the car—Jake'd be sharp enough to wonder about that."

Great-aunt shook her head impatiently. "You could run the car down around the bend in the road. He might not hear it start up there."

"He'd hear it," said Great-uncle flatly.

"Well, the wagon, then."

"All right," Great-uncle continued. "Say we got her in the wagon. Where we takin' her?"

"Why, she's got an uncle and aunt down in Prairie du Chien," said Great-aunt.

"Hoh! You don't expect us to drive down to Prairie du Chien in a wagon, Woman! By the time we got as far as Spring Green—before that, even—Jake'd be after us in his car."

Great-aunt looked vexed. "That's so," she agreed.

"If there was some way," said Gus apologetically, "we could sneak her inta Sac Prairie an' put her on the train, we could git her to Prairie du Chien, all right. The Milwaukee Road runs straight down there out a Mazomanie."

Great-aunt Lou brightened. "That's it," she cried, excitedly. "We could easy get her into Sac Prairie before Jake got too suspicious. It's only seven miles. We could even use the wagon."

Great-uncle refused to be stirred. "That means, on top a everything else, you got to git Molly and Jake over here about train time or jest before," he said. "It's gonna be hard enough to git 'em over here a-tall, let alone any special time."

Gus Elker's face fell. He looked the picture of woe. He had made his one contribution to the problem and his bosom friend had vetoed it. He seemed to shrink into his oversize overalls.

"We can do it," said Great-aunt confidently.

"Besides," Great-uncle went on, "you could trust Jake to think a the train. The minute he finds out she's gone, he'll be after that train. He could telegraph and have her taken off. She ain't of age, that's all there is to it."

Even Great-aunt Lou could not answer that argument.

"Unless," said Sim, "you found some way to hide her. On the train, I mean."

Great-uncle turned a dubious glance on Sim. "You better stick to harnesses, boy," he said. "How you gonna hide a grown girl who's a passenger on a train, I like to know? I be dog if it can be done."

"Be dog, then," said Sim. "You could put her in a box with holes in it and send her baggage, that's what you could do."

"That's right," I said.

Great-uncle Joe began to laugh. "Oh, I like to die if that ain't the craziest thing I heard yet!" he said, his great bulk shaking with his laughter.

Great-aunt Lou wasn't laughing, however. Neither was Gus Elker. Gus was getting a crafty expression on his face, the kind he got just about the time, out hunting, he was getting into position to aim a fatal shot at the fox he'd been trailing.

"That coffin," he said suddenly. "That coffin a Jake's."

"What about it?" asked Great-uncle.

"Don't they send coffins in a long-box?" asked Gus.

"Why, sure. Pine box, usually," said Great-aunt.

"An' one a them long-boxes is plenty big enough to stand up in. Real comfortable," said Gus hurriedly, before Great-uncle could dampen his enthusiasm. "We could git hold a that long-box Jake's coffin is comin' in, bore some holes in her, an' send it back with the train an' Molly in it, that's what we could do. It's all legal, too."

Great-uncle Joe made a last attempt to stem the enthusiasm Great-aunt Lou was beginning to share. "An' how we gonna git hold a that long-box, I like to know?"

Gus was daunted but for a few moments. "W'y," he said, sure of himself now, "we could meet the train an' collec' the coffin for Jake. Deliver it, too—on'y without the long-box."

"My, ain't that bright!" said Great-uncle sarcastically. "Right there at the depot with Mike Weinzierl and all the other depot loafers lookin' on. An' old Beau Wardler gittin' the mail to haul to the Post Office an' all."

"We don' have to go to the station," said Gus sullenly.

"How else you gonna git that coffin?"

"We can flag the train down jest where it comes over the bridge," said Gus. "It's dark there where it makes the bend to go round the canning factory, except for the streetlight at Mettel's old house—an' there ain't nobody livin' there now."

Great-uncle grinned. "An' how we gonna know when that coffin comes in?" he asked. "You figger old Porter'll call you up and let you know it's on the train?"

"No," said Gus hotly. "But he'll call Jake up, an' Jake's on my line, an' I can listen in."

"And you can call me, Gus," added Great-aunt Lou, "and as soon's you do, why, I'll telephone Jake to come over with Molly. He'll likely figure to leave her with us while he goes in for his coffin."

Great-uncle kept on grinning. "Ain't you all figurin' a little careless?" he wanted to know. "You keep talkin' about streetlights and dark—but what if that coffin comes in on the mornin' train?"

Gus began to wilt again. Great-aunt Lou looked flustered. Great-uncle's grin grew triumphant.

"Everybody in Sac Prairie knows most of the freight comes in on the evening train," I said. "Jake said he was getting his coffin out of Chicago. Practically all the Chicago freight comes in at night. I know." I did, too. I used to hang around the depot when Frankie Ackerman worked there for old Porter.

"That's when our harness leather comes, too," Sim put in.

"I reckon it's safe to figger it for the evenin' train," said Gus, cheered.

"It's the dumbest, foolishest thing I ever heard of," exploded Great-uncle. "It'll never work."

"Why not?" demanded Great-aunt.

"In the first place, I don't know whether it's legal," said Great-uncle, craftily aiming a shaft at Gus.

"How so? How so?" asked Gus quickly.

"What right we got to git Jake's coffin?"

"We're deliverin' it to him, ain't we? It ain't as if we was aimin' to steal it," protested Gus.

"Looks to me like we're stealin' his long-box."

Gus looked dismayed. This had not occurred to him.

"We're only borrowing it," put in Great-aunt.

"That's right," Gus agreed eagerly. "Once Molly's delivered safe an' sound in Prairie du Chien, we'll git it back for him."

"With holes in it," said Great-uncle.

"If it comes to that, I'll pay him for the holes," said Gus.

Sim began to laugh. I had to laugh, too.

Great-uncle appealed to us. "Ain't it crazy, Old Timer? You ever hear the like, Sim?" he wanted to know.

"Sure," I said, "it's crazy as all get-out! But what've you got to offer that's better?"

"Nothing," said Gus quickly. "He ain't said a thing but *no* ever' time his better half or I opened up."

"I guess Joe needn't to come," said Great-aunt. "Reckon he could set and talk to Jake while the rest of you snaked Molly out of the house and into town."

"Oh, no," cried Great-uncle. "That'd sure botch it up. Gus and the two kids! And that poor girl at the mercy a them! Why, Gus don't even know how to drive."

Gus yelped in protest. "Me not know how to drive? You ornery old coot, I druv a team long before you did."

"I had my car years before you had your'n," said Great-uncle.

"We ain't drivin' no car," said Gus flatly. "Ain't you forgittin' we got to sneak off an' git that coffin? We got to drive a wagon an' the team."

"You mean you want to come along on such a crazy trip?" asked Great-aunt Lou. "My conscience! that man a mine can't seem to decide which side he's on."

"I'm on Molly's side, same as the rest," said Great-uncle indignantly.

"All right, then," retorted Great-aunt. "I'll set on the porch and talk to Jake. The boys'll take Molly into the house and out the front door. You'll have the wagon all ready down around the bend. You and Gus'll have to make some excuse and go to the barn. You'll have to sneak out from there, so he don't see you."

Great-uncle Joe began to grin again. "You ain't even got him here yet," he said.

"We can't make our plans the last minute," protested Great-aunt. "We have to be ready."

"Well, I'm ready. I'm ready now. I'm ready for the biggest bust-up you ever did see," said Great-uncle. "Gus has come up with some dandies in my time, but this one beats 'em all, I like to die if it don't!"

Great-aunt Lou tried not to show that she was troubled.

Gus spoke bluntly. "I don't see how. You ain't helpin' none."

"It's got so many 'ifs' to it," explained Great-uncle. "If you catch the call Porter puts in to Jake. He'll notify him, I know he will—always does, when some large piece a express or freight comes in on the train. If Lou can talk Jake inta comin' over."

"That'll be easy," Great-aunt put in. "I'll tell him if he don't come over here, we're comin' over there. He won't want us there if he's got to git his coffin."

Great-uncle ignored her. "If he don't get suspicious before we're on our way and start out in his car for the depot."

"What if he does?" countered Great-aunt sharply. "You're heading for the railroad bridge, and he'll be heading for the depot more'n half a mile away."

"If we can flag down the train."

"I know Harry Jefferies real well," I said. "He'll stop her for me. See if he won't."

"If we can git that long-box an' coffin off the train."

"You have to sign for it, I guess," I said. "That's all. Maybe it's irregular, but they always do things easy-like. They don't fuss for the exact way to do it."

"If we can git Molly inta that box and back on the train," Great-uncle went on, just as if he had made up his mind to spoil Gus's plan. "It's all too many 'ifs' and we're bound to git caught on one of 'em. Jest suppose Jake's at the depot when the train gits there. He'll want that box. He'll holler to high heaven for that coffin."

"He'll git his coffin," said Gus doggedly.

"And you can wait and put the long-box with Molly in it on the train when it comes back," said Great-aunt tartly.

Sac Prairie was on the end of the spur from Mazomanie. The Milwaukee Road had put it in in 1881, and had meant to go on to Baraboo, but hadn't got around to doing it in time to keep the Northwestern from driving up by way of Lodi and Merrimac. So the trains that came into Sac Prairie just switched around a little, unloaded express, mail, and freight, loaded up again, and went back. The morning train had the big shipments going out, but the evening train usually went out half an hour or so after it came in. It would be easy to wait at the railroad bridge, and it would give us time to get Molly comfortably into the box.

"If—if—if—it's all 'if this' or 'if that'," said Great-uncle, bringing his fat hands heavily down to the tabletop, so that the dishes rattled. "It ain't gonna work."

"Nothin' works if you don't try it," said Gus.

"We'll try it," said Great-aunt with a settled air. "Till you think of something a good deal smarter, Joe, we'll try it. And if you don't like it, you just set here."

"Me? I wouldn't miss it," said Great-uncle Joe.

"And just to be on the safe side," continued Great-aunt Lou, "you'll have to keep close to that telephone, Gus. You'll have to be ready to go any time."

"I'm ready now," said Gus. "I ain't gonna have nobody forcin' no girl t' marry some man she don't want t' marry —not in my jurisdiction!"

Great-aunt Lou turned upon Great-uncle. "You, Joe— you settin' here all night? It's nine o'clock. It's about time you got out and gave Burl a hand."

Gus Elker hastily pushed back his chair, as if she had aimed a shaft at him. "I gotta git home, too," he said.

He got out of the kitchen ahead of Great-uncle Joe.

"And unless you boys're figuring to help with the dishes," continued Great-aunt, "you get out from under my feet, too."

We got out. Great-uncle had really riled her. I would have stayed, but I was against wiping dishes on principle. Hauling wood for the woodbox, feeding chickens, splitting and piling wood, even collecting the eggs—jobs like that were all right, but not sweeping up or washing or wiping dishes; those, I figured, were a woman's jobs, and a man oughtn't to have any part of them. Or boy, either. You had to draw the line somewhere, and that was where I drew it.

At home, helping with the dishes, sweeping, and ironing were my sister's chores, not mine.

We sat down on the edge of the porch. The waxing moon was bright in the southeastern sky, moving close to the full. The dark shadows of trees and buildings stretched out close to the trunks and walls in the farmyard. The cows had been turned out to night pasture, and the tinkling of the cowbell rode the night air. And in the woods the barred owls were making a racket that would die down as quickly as it had risen.

"What do you think, Steve?" asked Sim.

"Well, I guess that plan's all right as far as it goes," I said. "It doesn't go far enough."

"Those men," he said.

"That's right," I answered. "It doesn't take them into account. And I don't know but I think somewhere along the line we'll have to count them in."

14.

A Moonlight Sortie

I was still thinking about the men who watched Jake Riley's house when the clock struck midnight downstairs in the sleeping house. I was sitting up in bed, wondering whether those men were still keeping an eye on Jake's place, even at this hour. Moonlight lay in the parallelogram on the floor, pouring in at the south gable window, and Sim lay asleep. Everything was still.

I couldn't rest, for thinking and wondering, and at last I got out of bed and dressed. Sim heard me and woke up.

"What's the matter?" he whispered.

"I'm going out," I said. "Over to Jake Riley's."

"Good Gosh! What for?" He raised himself on one elbow.

"I want to find out whether those men are still watching Jake's place," I said.

"You couldn't see ten feet ahead of you in those woods," protested Sim.

"I don't plan to go into the woods," I answered. "I figure they're close in toward the house by night. Wouldn't you be, if you were watching a place? Not so close as to stir up the dog, but not so far off as to miss anybody coming to the house."

He swung his bony legs out of bed. "I'm going along."

"We have to get out the window," I said. "Auntie sleeps like a cat. She'll hear us on those creaky stairs."

"Pretty risky, isn't it?"

"We'll tie the sheets together and slide down the back porch roof," I said.

Sim started to dress. By the time he had got into his clothes, I had the sheets off the bed and was hard at work. There was enough moonlight reflected in the room to see by. Sim kept looking around for a place to tie on to, but I figured the bed would hold us, if we went down one by one. It was a big, old-fashioned double bed, buttressed on the north side by an old square bureau. It would take a lot to pull it loose.

I tied the end of one sheet to the near leg of the bed and threw the other out the north gable window.

"I'll test her," said Sim.

"No," I said. "If it'll hold me, it'll hold you, but it won't necessarily hold me if you get down it all right."

I braced myself and pulled hard on the sheets we had tied together. The bed didn't budge. I climbed up on the window ledge, squeezed through the window, and sort of walked backward down the wall, holding myself by means of the sheet. When I came to the end I could just touch the roof of the porch with my toes. Sim was watching anxiously. When he saw that I had reached the roof, he climbed out, too.

I walked over the roof and swung myself off the edge, so

that I wouldn't make much noise when I dropped to the ground. I waited there for a few moments.

Then Sim came.

I started out up the lane toward the pasture and the woods looming dark in the moonlight to the east.

"You're going away from Riley's place," said Sim, catching up.

"I know what I'm doing," I said.

"I wonder. Good Gosh! Going on one o'clock in the morning!" he grumbled.

"Did you ever see a nicer night?" I asked.

It *felt* like one o'clock in the morning. Just about everything was still. Down toward the Ferry Bluff a fox barked. Way up high in the air there was a sound like swallows twittering. It was a sound I had heard several times in Sac Prairie at night, and during storms, but I couldn't tell where it came from. Perhaps it *was* swallows. It came down like fine, faraway music. Far, far to the south, a train whistle made its lonesome call. There was nothing else.

Moonlight lay on the ground like sunlight seen through dark glasses. It made the pasture almost as light as day. It lay up against the woods, and filtered in among the trees. Here and there in the woods it shone in open places like foxfire. The moon was over in the southwestern sky now, beginning to slide down toward the western rim. It was so bright it dimmed the stars. Only Antares shone near it, and Vega high over.

We made hardly a sound where we walked, except for Sim's grumbling.

"Maybe," he said, once we had begun to go through the woods, "we're finally going fishing."

"Listen," I said, "you can go back any time you feel like it. I didn't tell you to come. You made up your own mind."

"But why're you going east when Jake Riley lives north of your uncle's place?" he demanded.

"Why, Sim, I want to come in along the road. If somebody's watching, they'll be sure to see me."

"What if they do?"

"I want to find out what happens."

Sim thought this over for about ten steps. Then he said, "Well, your uncle isn't the only crazy one in your family."

"He sure isn't," I agreed.

Sim just sniffed.

We went on through the woods, under a fence, through some more woods, and came out at last on the Skunk Hollow road. It ribboned away to the north in the moonlit landscape, but to the south along the woods it was dark. I was ready to follow the road north to where it turned through a cut and went west, almost directly facing Jake Riley's place, when Sim caught hold of my arm.

"Look there," he said.

I looked to where he pointed. South of us a logging road cut into the woods. About two hundred feet up the road something shone in the moonlight.

"There's a car hid there," said Sim.

"Sure is," I agreed. "It might be some kids out necking, but I don't think so."

"Not there," said Sim. "Ferry Bluff, maybe—but not there."

I turned. "I'm going to look."

Sim stood where he was. He was undecided. He didn't know who might come out of the car ready to fight. But he didn't want me to face him alone, either. So he came up behind me. I could feel his reluctance.

"How much you bet it's the same car we saw at the peaviner that day?" I whispered.

"I'm not betting," he said.

It wasn't the same car. It was empty. I put my hand on the hood. It was cold. It had been standing there a while. I tried the door. It wasn't locked. I opened the door and looked in. There wasn't light enough to see much by. There wasn't anything I could see in the car.

"You going to take the license down?" asked Sim.

I shook my head. "I'd bet money on it this is another one of those Rent-a-Car Agency cars."

We left the car and started up the Skunk Hollow road toward the cut.

"One of us," I said, "can walk up the road and into the drive to Jake's place. But not two. I'm the one. You stay at the cut."

"Why me?"

"One of us has to see what happens," I said. "What if I get shot? Who'd know it, if you weren't there?"

Sim cleared his throat nervously.

"Unless you want to go ahead," I said.

"You just go," said Sim.

The cut was a place where the Skunk Hollow road passed between two walls of limestone. On top of the walls grew dense woods. From the edge of the woods on the west side, you could look down into Skunk Hollow. You could see all the way up to Jake Riley's place, and all the way up to the end of the Hollow, where the Witwen road went by. You could even see the peaviner station from there, and that was the first thing we saw when we got to the cut.

There was another car standing there. It could be seen plainly in the moonlight. It wouldn't have been visible from Jake Riley's place up in the Pocket.

"We're surrounded," whispered Sim.

"Uh-huh," I agreed. "I figured at least two men watching Jake's place. Now I guess there might be more."

"What's going on?"

"I wish I could tell," I said. "About the only thing I'm sure of is they're not watching Molly." I added, "Nor Jake. He hardly moves out of the house."

I had some misgivings about what I planned to do. Sight of that second car was a little unsettling. I had to tell myself that the Baker Street Irregulars wouldn't have backed out now; so the Mill Creek Irregulars couldn't, either.

"I'm going," I said.

"Maybe you'd better not," said Sim.

That was all I needed to shove me. "You watch," I said. "If anything happens to me . . ."

"Like what?"

"Oh, if I'm picked up and carried off," I said.

Sim tittered. "It'd have to be a big man to do it. Used to lifting weights."

"The trouble with you is nothing's sacred," I said, a little griped.

"Imagine carrying you away," said Sim. "It'd be a lot easier just to crack you one and let you lie."

"You come along and bring me to, if it happens," I said.

I left him.

I went down the middle of the road, out of the shadows of the cut, into the moonlight. The moon was just ahead of me. Its light seemed to be pooled in the Skunk Hollow. It shone from the windows of Jake Riley's house. It shone from the windows of the houses up the Hollow, like fire. A dog barked up the Hollow, and two others, including Jake Riley's dog, took up the barking. But before I had gone very far, the dogs were quiet again.

Down where the Skunk Hollow road turned north once more, Jake Riley's gravel drive made a moonlit lane up into the Pocket. Right there, just past the entrance to the driveway, stood a big clump of young poplar trees. It was dark and thick. It was just the place for somebody to hide. You couldn't see much of Jake Riley's house from it—just the porch and the door opening off it—but you could certainly see the whole Skunk Hollow road from the cut to the north end, and all the driveway which led into the Riley farmyard.

I wouldn't be able to walk much farther than the poplar grove, anyway, I reasoned. By the time I got about half a block from it, the dog would be able to hear me on the gravel.

Walking along that road at one o'clock in the morning was like walking out of this world. Not even a breeze stirred the hot August night. Not a mosquito was out. They had crowded the evening, but now, at this hour, they had gone to grass and to hang on to the under side of leaves until the next evening. The night was so still that even the little gravel I scuffed, careful as I was, sounded like thunder rolling down the Baraboo bluffs.

I got to the driveway. I stood there and looked around.
I sort of hesitated to go any farther. But if anybody were
watching the Riley place, the poplar grove would be just
about the only place close by from which to do it. I had
to go past that, at least.

I started up the driveway with especial care, because
I didn't want to alert Jake's dog.

I got in just past the poplar grove when something
came up against my back.

And somebody said, "Put up your hands!"

My hands went up so fast anybody who'd have seen
me would have thought I was grabbing for the moon. I
just froze right there. My pulse shot up to about a hundred within a second or two, and two breaths later, it
must have been crowding a hundred fifty. I knew what
was pressing into my back. It was a gun. Judging by how
close the fellow who held it was standing, it must have
been a pistol.

The pressure went off.

"Turn around. Slow."

I turned around. Now that I hadn't been shot, I began
to think again. I knew that voice. I had heard that voice
only a few days ago. There was that pistol looking me in
the face. The man who held it, I could see by the moonlight, was the same fellow who had been around making
surveys not very long ago.

"Why Mr. Barton!" I said. "Kind of late for a survey,
isn't it?"

Even in the moonlight, I could see how disgusted he
looked. His gun sort of wilted away. He put it back into
his pocket.

"What in the world are you doing out here at this hour of the night?" he demanded.

"Mr. Barton," I said, "sometimes I walk in my sleep. I'm that worried about Molly Burns, I must have dreamed about her and got up and walked over to see if she was all right."

I said all this with a straight face. Mr. Barton didn't know what to think. He just stared at me.

"And what are you surveying tonight?" I asked.

"Boy," he said slowly, "too much curiosity is a bad thing."

"That's not what my Grandpa says," I said. "If you don't ask questions, you'll never learn anything."

"Boy," said Mr. Barton, "go home."

"Mr. Barton," I said earnestly, "maybe I could help you some. Are you lost?"

"No, I'm not lost."

"If it's a special kind of survey you're making," I said, "I'm pretty good at surveys myself. I can name just about any star up there in the sky. I know most of the birds around here. And snakes," I said, "you just ask me. That poplar grove, for instance, could be dangerous. And you oughtn't to be running around here with leather-soled shoes on. You're apt to slip on the hill slopes."

Mr. Barton, I could see, would have liked to shake me up. "Boy," he said again, "you just run along. You go home and stop walking around in your sleep. Not that I believe it."

"You have to have faith in people, Mr. Barton," I said. "Maybe even in Jake Riley."

I shouldn't have said that. One of my troubles has always been that I only know what I shouldn't have said when it's popped out of my mouth. Mr. Barton sort of stiffened.

"How long has that curiosity of yours been functioning?" he asked. "You'll poke your nose out too far some day and get it cut off."

"Oh, I've been curious since I was born," I said. "It's been a great problem for Pa and Ma."

"I can believe it," said Barton. "Now, get going."

I didn't wait to be invited again. I went back out of the driveway and up the road. I looked back once. Mr. Barton had faded from sight. I knew he was in the poplar grove again. I knew he'd be there until just about dawn. Then he'd high-tail it back to his car. Where the other fellow was I didn't know, but I was sure he was somewhere around.

Sim came sliding down the side of the cut as I came up to it.

"What happened?" he asked. "What went on down there? I saw that fellow."

I told him as we walked on.

"Barton!" he exclaimed. "And with a gun!"

"It wasn't a stick," I said. "A pistol. Colt, I thought. Maybe a Smith & Wesson."

Over in the southwest now the moon was lowering, growing a deeper yellow. I hoped we could get into the house the same way we went out. I hoped Great-aunt Lou wouldn't notice how we had used her sheets.

"Steve," said Sim in a troubled voice. "This is serious. This is something big—bigger than Molly being locked up or Molly getting married or Molly's money."

"I know it," I said, "but I still don't know what it's all about."

"George," said Sim.

"Sure, George. I grant that—maybe with a reservation or two. But why?"

And that was saying just about all that could be said. It summed up where we stood.

"If those fellows are watching Jake like this, what'll happen when we try to get Molly out?" Sim wanted to know.

"I don't know that it's Jake they're interested in," I answered. "It's Jake's house. It's that place. It's not Jake —but somebody else. Whoever it was Barton was asking about that day, and that other fellow in the woods was looking for."

"George," said Sim again.

"Sure," I said. "But right now we take first things first. And Molly comes first. Once we get her out of the way, we can start worrying about George."

"You scared?" asked Sim.

"Scared!" I said. "I can still feel that gun pushed up into my back!"

15.

We Act upon Our Plan

THAT next afternoon my Great-uncle Arnold Stoll and Great-aunt Annie came visiting. Great-uncle Arnold was even bigger than Great-uncle Joe. He stood about half a head higher, and the fat on him was raised up, half on his chest and half on his stomach, not down low, like Great-uncle Joe's. He was long-legged, and he walked with a sort of stoop—that kind of stoop tall people sometimes put on because they are self-conscious about their height. He always wore a black, broad-brimmed felt hat. His face was rounder than Great-uncle Joe's, and his eyes were merrier. His cheeks were rosy, and his broad mouth was almost covered by a thick, straggly moustache. By contrast, Great-aunt Annie was rail-thin, with a slender, almost drawn face, and a high-pitched voice that contrasted with her husband's booming.

When they drove into the yard, we were all in the barn. Burl and Great-uncle Joe were milking the cows, and Great-aunt Lou was standing there fretting about Molly Burns. Hearing the car drive in, Great-aunt went out of the barn.

"Half an hour earlier," she said, "and you'd have been in time to help with the milking."

"We been to see Lizzie," said Great-uncle Arnold. "How're you folks all?"

"We can't stay," added Great-aunt Annie.

"Stay at least for supper," said Great-aunt Lou. "Come along, Annie—you can help get it on."

They got out of the car—she to follow Great-aunt Lou, and he to join the others in the barn. We trailed along back into the barn and sat astride one of the stanchions to listen to the hearty talk they made—of Grandmother Adams, of "Adams"—as they called Grandfather, of Mother and Father, of how things were at Great-uncle Arnold's farm, which was in a little valley beside a cool spring about halfway between Spring Green and Lone Rock—and there we sat until Great-aunt Lou's strident voice announced supper.

We were still at the supper table when Gus Elker came. It was a little after seven, with the sun not yet below the horizon, the birds singing for evening, and the first nighthawks sky-coasting, when he came bursting into the kitchen, out of breath because he had run all the way from his place.

"That coffin a Jake's is comin' by tonight's train," he cried. "Due nine-thirty or there'bouts. An' Jake's figgerin' on meetin' the train to git it."

"Jukas!" exclaimed Great-uncle Joe, and came to his feet so violently that he almost upset the table.

"We'll have to git the wagon ready," said Gus. "And a lantern with a red cloth around it . . ."

Great-uncle Arnold and Great-aunt Annie sat, mouths agape, in astonishment at this performance.

"What in tarnation's up?" asked Great-uncle Arnold.

Great-aunt Lou rose and went to the wall telephone. She called Jake Riley. It took a while for Jake to answer, and when he did it was plain from what Great-aunt said that he didn't take kindly to her invitation to come over for the evening. Nor to her insistence.

"If you can't come, Jake, we'll come over there," she said finally.

This must have needled him. Great-aunt stood listening for quite a while, a tight smile on her lips. Then she spoke again.

"Well, you just come over, Jake, and when you and Molly have to go to town, you just go ahead. Or you can leave Molly with us and pick her up when you come back."

There was some further talk from Jake, but at last Great-aunt Lou's satisfaction showed on her face. She hung up.

"He's comin' over with Molly," she said. "And you come mighty handy, Arnold. You might just set a spell and help us entertain Jake Riley when he gets here."

"Is that old sinner still alive?" asked Great-uncle Arnold, grinning. "I ain't seen him for nigh on to three years."

"He's alive, all right," said Gus Elker.

Great-aunt Annie sat sharp-faced. "Something's up here," she said. "What is it?"

"The men're aiming to pick up Jake Riley's coffin that he's sent for, and fetch it out," said Great-aunt Lou matter-of-factly. "They want to surprise him."

"We ought to be getting home, Arnold," said Great-aunt Annie.

"Might's well stay to see Jake," said Great-uncle Joe.

His brother nodded. "Always seemed to me something queer about that feller. He don't seem *right* to me, somehow."

"We got work to do," Great-uncle Joe burst out. "Old Timer, you and Sim git that lantern set. Gus an' me'll harness up the horses and git the wagon down the road around the bend, so's we'll be all ready."

"We're fixing to get Molly away from Jake," my Great-aunt Lou explained. "Jake's aiming to marry her off to his nephew from Chicago, and I don't see Molly doing that of her own free will."

Great-aunt Annie was immediately indignant. "That fat old toad!" she cried. "We'll surely stay to help."

Great-uncle Joe and Gus Elker went out, refusing Great-uncle Arnold's offer of help. Sim and I went out, too. We knew where the lantern was, and the red cloth had been dug out by Great-aunt Lou—a piece of her checkered kitchen tablecloth—so everything was ready for us.

Great-uncle and Gus worked themselves into a lather getting the horses out of the pasture and into harness. You'd have thought Jake Riley was due any second. Sim and I had the lantern ready in only a few minutes; then we lent a hand.

"Now we gotta git her set around the bend," said Gus.

"Hold on," I said. "We can't take the wagon there yet."

"Why not, I like to know?" demanded Great-uncle.

"If Jake's coming around intending to go into Sac

Prairie for his coffin, he'll have the truck," I said. "He'll come past the wagon. It might make him suspicious."

"That's right," agreed Gus. "I be dog if I never thought a that. Now what'll we do?"

Great-uncle looked blank.

"Couldn't we take the wagon down to the Fair Valley Store?" asked Sim.

"Too far," decided Great-uncle at once. "We have to be on the way before we could git Molly all the way down there—afoot from here." He shook his head and his jowls shook, too. "No, we'll have to have it closer'n that to the house."

"How about in the woods?" asked Sim.

"Too thick," said Great-uncle.

Gus Elker's sad face lit up. "Say, remember that ol' cabin up on the south hill?" he asked suddenly. "The road . . ."

Great-uncle took up his words, cutting him off. "That's right—there's an old road still there at that place. We might have to chop down a small tree or two—but that's jest the ticket!"

Great-uncle Joe and Gus climbed into the wagon and mounted to the seat, while Sim and I jumped into the box. Great-uncle started the horses. We rattled out of the yard down the drive toward the highway. Gus kept his eyes fixed on the side of the road.

Just around the bend south of the house, and out of sight and sound of it, Gus pointed. "There!" he shouted. "There's what's left a that road."

Great-uncle drew the horses up.

What looked like unbroken woods did show now a long-abandoned road, scarcely to be seen. I would never have seen it, if Gus hadn't pointed it out.

"One or two trees!" exclaimed Sim sarcastically.

There were no less than seven small trees in the way. Great-uncle had thrown two axes into the wagon-box. He and Gus each grabbed one and began to chop. Sim and I dragged the trees back into the woods, out of sight and out of the way of the wagon, as fast as the men cut them down. It seemed a shame to cut out all those young trees, but there was nothing else to be done.

It took us twenty minutes to clear the old road. Then, when the horses and wagon had been driven up into it, they were still too easy to see, if anybody driving up along the road to Great-uncle Joe's place were to turn and look over his shoulder. Sim and I had to drag out two of the trees and stand them up in the abandoned road to conceal the wagon. Only then did we feel it safe to return to the house.

We had just settled ourselves on the back porch, when Jake Riley and Molly drove in. Jake was driving his truck, all right. He was figuring on going in to Sac Prairie for his coffin.

"It's going to be close," muttered Sim dubiously. "This is the craziest thing yet."

"Fun, though," I said.

Jake backed out of his truck, and the truck shook and creaked with each step he took, moving all his weight. He was grumbling as Molly descended from the other side.

"What's your trouble, Jake?" Great-aunt Lou hollered at him.

"My coffin's comin' in," he answered. "I ought to go

down and get it off the train tonight. She's due nine-thirty."

"Hoh! You ain't dyin' yet," she called back, "and that coffin can wait. You can get it after they unload it."

"Porter don't stay there all night," protested Jake. "And I don't plan to load it up all by myself."

"Joe can go along and help," promised Great-aunt.

Jake came up through the twilight to the porch, his immense bulk dwarfing even Great-uncle Arnold, whom Jake now saw for the first time.

"Well, if it ain't Arnold!" he said.

"You still the same lazy old devil?" asked Great-uncle Arnold.

I looked over at Molly, who had come up behind her stepfather. She sat down at Great-aunt Lou's side, timidly acknowledging the presence of my Great-aunt Annie. Her eyes were fixed half fearfully on her stepfather's dark figure, for the sun was now long lost behind the hills, and even the afterglow was drawing down from the zenith. Whippoorwills were singing out of the deepening dusk of Stone's Pocket.

Great-uncle Arnold and Jake began to reminisce, while the darkness came in. After a little while, Great-uncle Joe got up with a great show of apology.

"I better look at that mare a mine," he said. He added to Jake, "I got a sick horse down in the back pasture."

He walked away, promising to be back.

"I reckon I'll come, too," said Gus, and started after him.

"I'll just sit here," said Jake. "No sense to me moving all this meat around if I don't have to."

Everyone laughed, including Jake.

A few more minutes passed. Then, seeing that Great-uncle Arnold had engaged Jake Riley in animated conversation, Great-aunt Lou turned to Molly and spoke.

"Might be you and the boys could find something to do in the house," she said.

"Sure," I chimed in. "We got a telescope in the attic. We could look at the stars."

"I think I'd like that," said Molly eagerly.

Jake looked around sharply. "Don't go far, girl," he said with an edge to his tongue. "We got to be getting into town. You mind, now."

"No," said Molly meekly.

Great-aunt Lou got up. "I'll just go along and light the way. There's no electricity upstairs."

She led the way into the kitchen. I could feel Jake Riley's eyes on our backs, but Great-uncle Arnold's questions commanded his attention. Great-aunt went to the lamp and lit it. She carried it out of the kitchen, and the minute the door was shut behind her, she turned on Molly.

"Molly, do you *want* to marry Jake's nephew?" she demanded.

"Oh, no!" cried Molly. "I want to get away. *He* won't let me. He keeps me locked in my room sometimes."

"You want to go to Prairie du Chien to your uncle and aunt?"

"Oh, I want to, I want to!" cried Molly.

It just made me sick to see how soft she was. If we didn't get her away, she'd do just what Jake wanted, she was that scared of him. She never fought back once, I'd have bet.

"Enough to go down in a box?" asked Great-aunt.

Molly looked at her in wide-eyed wonder, but she nodded.

"Then go with the boys, quick, now."

She put down the lamp and returned through the kitchen to the back porch.

Molly and Sim and I moved through the front room, out the front door, and down to the road as fast and as quietly as we could. We never made a sound, outside of one board on the front steps that creaked when I stepped on it. Molly didn't ask a question. She just came along. She was so scared, and so used to doing as she was told, that she just trusted us blindly.

Great-uncle Joe and Gus Elker had the wagon backed out into the road by the time we got there. Neither one said a word. We helped Molly into the wagon-box, and the three of us sat down behind the seat. Great-uncle started up the horses—at first slowly, then, as we got down to the highway, much faster.

"It's eight-thirty, a little better," said Great-uncle Joe then. "How come you took so long, Old Timer?"

"Gosh, it was only a few minutes," I said. "Auntie had to get Molly into the house and find out what she wanted."

Great-uncle turned and peered at Molly.

"I want to get away," said Molly.

"That's what we figured," said Great-uncle.

"I known it all along," said Gus, with obvious self-satis-faction. "I tol' you right off something was wrong over at Jake's place, but you didn' b'lieve me."

Great-uncle affected not to hear him. He explained to

Molly just what he had in mind, telling her about the long-box and how she would be shipped in it.

"Couldn't I just take the train?" asked Molly. She wasn't much impressed with Great-uncle Joe's plan.

"We figger your steppa could have you took off," Gus explained. "Seein' as how you ain't of age."

"I'll be eighteen next week," said Molly.

Great-uncle turned around sharply. "We figgered Jake'd have you married off by that time," he said. "Ain't George about due?"

"He's *been* due. Jake told me George would be coming in any day now; he's said it all month long."

"Well, you ain't gonna marry nobody you ain't a mind to," promised Great-uncle firmly. "Not if I can help it."

Molly didn't say anything, but we could almost feel her gratitude. Nobody spoke. The wagon rattled over the bridge below the falls of the millpond, and around past the mill. The night was clear and warm. The moon was in the east, almost full; long shadows stretched across the road—of old willow trees and birch and poplar groves. The whippoorwills were still now, but owls called out of the dark Mill Bluff, and wood ducks along the creek, and nighthawks coasted down the sky over the pond, and kill-deers flew crying over the fields.

Great-uncle turned up the Lower Mill Road. The dusty air was sweet and cloying with the musk of corn. Except where water stood or ran, you could hardly smell anything but corn and dust. Now and then the pungence of mares-tails rose from the roadside, but that was all. We rode steadily up the Lower Mill Road, bouncing over the old bridge across the Otter Creek, and mounting the little rise beyond it. From there we could see the lights of Sac Prairie, all yellow along the eastern horizon, pale under the bright moon.

All of a sudden, Sim poked me.

I leaned around Molly and glared at him.

He just pointed behind us.

I looked back along the road. At first I didn't see anything. Then I saw the dim lights of a car. I watched them. After a while they went out. I kept on watching. The lights came on again. The car didn't seem to catch up to us.

"I saw 'em first just near the Mill Creek bridge," said Sim. "I reckon we're being followed."

"Could it be Jake?"

Molly stirred. "No. One of the headlights on the truck is bad. It flickers. Those lights aren't like the truck's."

"A car could catch up and pass us easy," said Sim. "Whoever's driving that one don't want to. Just watch it. You'll see."

I watched.

Sim was right. The car came on a way, then slowed up. Maybe the car just stopped. Maybe it came along without lights. The moonlight was bright enough to drive by.

"I can figure who that might be," I said. "But why would they be following us? It's Jake and Jake's place they've been watching. I don't catch on to this."

Sim didn't say anything. I noticed his one hand moving along the side of the wagon-box.

"What's the matter?" I asked.

Sim sort of cleared his throat, uneasily. "Feels like a gun is here beside me," he said.

"A gun!" I cried, remembering Grandfather Adams' warning about Great-uncle and Gus carrying guns.

Gus Elker came to life. He turned around, a broad smile on his face. "I brung me my shotgun along," he said. "You never can tell what happens."

"That Gus," said Great-uncle, "is always lookin' for trouble."

"I got the law on my side. I'm the law," said Gus. "I'm the Justice a the Peace."

"Ain't you forgittin' Sac Prairie's outa your district?" asked Great-uncle.

"I be dog if I didn' forgit that," admitted Gus.

He didn't sound repentant.

Behind us the car was still coming slowly along. Crawling—hardly more.

"I don't know about you," said Sim, "but I feel cold."

I felt cold all over.

16.

George

WHERE it came into town along the Wisconsin, the Lower Mill Road turned north. Only about two blocks from the place where it turned was the railroad crossing just off the bridge. There was only one house between the turn and the crossing—set just about halfway. The next house was the empty one where the bridge-tender used to live next to the tracks. West of there was an old abandoned factory building, and up along the tracks, where they turned north after coming in from the east across the bridge, was the canning factory, where I worked sometimes in summer, making the brine for the peas. There was one streetlight at the corner, and there was another one right off the crossing.

The car that was following us drew up a little closer after we got into Sac Prairie, but the men who were in it must have missed us when we turned into the yard of the old factory there west of the bridge, for the car went right past under the streetlight and on up into town.

I looked at Sim. "Mistake?" I guessed. "They missed us."

Sim shook his head pessimistically. "Not a chance."

Great-uncle stopped the wagon next to the tracks almost in the shadow of the old factory building.

"What time is it?" asked Gus.

Great-uncle lit a match and pulled his heavy watch out of his pocket. "Quarter past nine," he said. "She's about due."

"Lissen for the whistle at Heiney's Crossing," said Gus. "She'll be whistlin' any minute now."

For a few moments everyone was expectantly still. From the direction of the bridge came the music of the water around the piers where the Wisconsin went by on its way to the Mississippi below Prairie du Chien. The water's hushing was a cool, pleasant sound. It reminded me of days and nights on the river. It made me think of all the fishing Sim and I missed. It made me think of that raft trip we had taken down river two months before.

Herons called from the bars, where they were foraging in the shallow water. Killdeers cried along the river's edge, and sandpipers' shrill calls rose now and then. I could smell the musk of the river even back here, five hundred feet away. The river musk and the smell of the old factory and the stench of decaying peavines from the canning factory north of us, and the heady perfume of corn in fields west of us were all mixed together.

Sim leaned over and whispered, "I don't know what we're doing here, Steve. If we had any sense, we'd get out and go home. The more I think about this, the cooler I get."

"This is the Mill Creek Irregulars' first case," I said. "We have to stick with it."

"I got a feeling we're going to get stuck," retorted Sim, raising his voice a little. "Maybe this is kidnapping."

Gus Elker turned around. "Who's kidnappin'?" he wanted to know. "Kidnappin' is where somebody's took without their consent. Molly gave her consent."

"Shut up," growled Great-uncle Joe. "A body couldn't hear the train whistle with all this talk."

Just then the locomotive whistled. The long drawn-out whistle rose sweetly out of the south. It made a lonesome sound. Old 1040 with Harry Jefferies driving her. The whistle rose and fell three times.

"Git that lantern ready," said Gus.

I handed him the lantern.

He lit two matches, but he was too excited to light the lantern. Great-uncle grabbed it from him and lit it himself. He handed it back to me.

"You take it, Old Timer," he said.

From Heiney's Crossing the train had to come up a good mile before the Spring Slough, where it curved over a long trestle and turned west to cross the two bridges—the one over the east channel of the Wisconsin, the second over the main channel, which ended at the road off which we had just turned.

I got out of the wagon with the lantern and walked back along the tracks a little way. There I stood, hoping nobody would drive along the road and see me. The old bridge-tender's deserted house hid me from view of anybody in Sac Prairie, which lay north of the tracks, and in the house on the south no light burned.

I felt uneasy. What if Harry didn't see me? I had better not stand on the tracks, but just off to the side, in case he missed me. I could feel everybody waiting behind me. Out of the marshes east of the river came the rumbling of the train. There would be at least two coaches with perhaps a few drummers in them. There would be any number of freight cars and stock cars. The stock cars would be empty. The coaches would be next to the caboose at the end of the train. The baggage car would be just behind the engine. I hoped there were enough freight cars between the baggage car and the coaches to keep anybody in the coaches from knowing what was going on up in front. The way I figured it, the coaches would be stopped out on the bridge.

The locomotive's headlight swung around the Spring Slough Trestle a good half mile east of where I stood. It sort of hypnotized me. The whistle began to sound again. The headlight grew bigger as the locomotive hit the first span of the east channel bridge, and the rumbling rolled up like thunder. I was so fascinated by that oncoming headlight I just stood there until I heard Great-uncle's anxious whistle behind me, sharp and meaningful.

I began to swing the lantern with the red tablecloth around it.

The train came on, across Bergen's Island, on to the west channel bridge. The train normally slowed for the crossing, and it was slowing now. I couldn't tell whether Harry had seen me or not. He should have seen the lantern. I kept on swinging it. It began to look as if the train would rush right past me, when I heard the brakes being set.

The locomotive passed me, slowing, just about as I figured it would. The coaches, I could see, would be just out on the bridge off Bergen's Island. The conductor couldn't get up front, and nobody back there could see what was going on.

The train jarred to a stop, creaking and complaining. Every car all the way back seemed to stop separately, one after the other. There stood the locomotive, steaming and hissing, a great cloud of smoke pouring from its funnel.

I ran back, pulling the red cloth off the lantern.

Harry Jefferies was coming down from the engine, and the fireman was leaning out. Harry saw me.

"What's going on here?" shouted Harry. His face was troubled. He looked at me with his eyes wide and alarmed. "You, Steve! What's the trouble?"

I waved toward the wagon. Great-uncle Joe had got off. So had the others. Gus Elker was carrying his shotgun.

"Harry, we had to do it," I said. "We had to get Jake Riley's coffin off."

Harry just stared at me. I guess he thought I was out of my mind. "A half mile from the depot," he said, as if he couldn't believe this had happened to him.

Great-uncle Joe came up. "Jake needs it," he said.

Harry's face lengthened. I figured he thought Jake had died. "It ain't the right way to do it," he muttered. "But I guess it can be done. You have to sign for it."

"I'll sign," said Great-uncle.

A brakeman came up. Along the top of the freight cars came the conductor. I had underestimated him. He swung his gangly legs down the side of the baggage car and dropped to the ground.

"What'd you stop for, Harry?" he hollered.

Harry explained.

The conductor looked at us. Two men, two boys, and a girl. He saw the wagon.

"Coffin!" he said. "Can't he wait? Is he dead?"

"Not yet," said Gus lugubriously. His voice suggested that Jake's death was but a matter of seconds.

For a moment the conductor's decision hung on a thread. Then he shrugged and said, "Come along."

He went to the baggage car. The brakeman held up his lantern. Up ahead the locomotive still hissed, and the smoke from the stack glowed red in the reflection from the firebox.

The conductor opened the baggage car. The long-box stood ready for immediate unloading. The brakeman swung into the car, setting his lantern on the floor. Great-uncle moved forward to lend a hand, Gus at his heels. The conductor joined the brakeman in the car.

"Careful," he warned. "She's pretty heavy."

"We can take her all right," Great-uncle assured him.

The long-box with the coffin inside came sliding out of the car to the ground. It took noticeable effort on the part of Great-uncle and Gus to hold up the portion of the weight that was theirs.

The brakeman and the conductor jumped from the car. The brakeman slid the door shut once more.

"You can sign for it at the depot tomorrow morning," said the conductor. "Pay the charges then. The bill'll be there."

Gus Elker pressed forward. "We're aimin' t' send the box back with a body in it," he said.

The conductor just shrugged.

"Tonight yet," said Great-uncle Joe.

The conductor gave him a long hard look. "You said Jake Riley wasn't dead yet. What's this?"

"Not Jake," said Gus.

Great-uncle took alarm. He pulled Gus back and said, "If we got anything to ship out, we'll be at the depot with it."

"I'd think so," said the conductor.

He climbed up the baggage car like a monkey and ran back out on the bridge across the tops of the freight and stock cars. The fireman climbed back in, and Harry Jefferies followed him. He leaned out of the cab waiting for the brakie's swinging lantern to signal him to go ahead. It came.

The locomotive chuffed and began to move. Cinders came down over us in a fine dust. The train lurched forward, gathering speed as the locomotive pulled ahead. The cars went by, one after the other, and at last the caboose flashed past, its red and green lights dwindling up the tracks as it swung past the canning factory toward the station half a mile ahead.

We were alone with the long-box. It looked strange and a little sombre in the glow of the lantern.

"That's heavier'n I figgered on," said Great-uncle. "I didn' know coffins come that heavy."

"We better git that thing open an' the coffin out," said Gun nervously. "I ain't exac'ly likin' it here. I be dog if I don't feel like I was in a cemetery. You brung a hammer an' chisel, didn' you, Joe?"

Great-uncle nodded. He walked back to the wagon and got a hammer and chisel out from under the seat.

Gus was examining the long-box. "Funny thing," he said, as Great-uncle came up. "Looks t' me there's holes fixed in her a'ready. Save us a lot a trouble."

Great-uncle stopped where he was. He reached over and took the lantern out of my hand. He held it up.

Sure enough, there were augur holes in the long-box.

Sim looked at me, and I looked at Sim. I had a funny feeling low down in my stomach.

Gus grabbed the hammer and chisel and got to work. The cover of the long-box came off in no time at all. There lay the coffin—a pearl gray and bronze creation. It was unusually large, but it had to be, for Jake Riley had had it made to order.

"Are them holes, too?" asked Gus, pointing.

He had leveled his forefinger at strange-looking slits along the sides of the coffin. They looked like gills opening into the coffin. Great-uncle Joe stared at them with a queer, baffled expression on his face.

"Be dog if they ain't," he said.

"A man don't breathe any more in his coffin," said Gus.

He bent over the coffin to take a closer look.

At that instant, the coffin's cover flew up. A man came up with it, a revolver in one hand. He stood there, looking wildly around—a hard-looking man of about thirty, dark and mean-faced. The shock of his appearance was so great that Gus fell over backward and the long-box cover came down on top of him. Great-uncle stepped back and dropped his tools. Sim just shrank farther back into the shadows, while Molly froze in her tracks. I had a wild impulse to take to my heels and fly for home.

"Thanks," the fellow said. "I got out sooner than I expected." He waved his gun around. "Now don't any of you make a move, or you'll pick up lead."

He spoke too late. The first access of terror that had seized Gus had passed. His first impulse now was to get at his shotgun. He rolled out from under the long-box cover, fell upon his weapon, and, before any of us realized his intention, he had discharged it into the night with a deafening roar.

The man in the coffin slanted his revolver and shot out the lantern light.

At the same moment, a bullet came singing out of the dark behind my Great-uncle. A voice shouted, "Put 'em up, George!"

Another voice called, "Look out for the old men and the kids!"

George leaped out of the coffin and long-box.

Great-uncle Joe fell to his knees and hit the ground with his belly. "Drop, Old Timer," he hollered. "Somebody's shootin'!"

Sim and I were down long before he had opened up. I had pulled Molly down on top of us. And Gus had just stayed down.

The whole night seemed to explode. A fusillade of shots punctured the darkness. Shouts rang out, shots cracked, bullets sang. The sounds of a wild chase echoed through the moonlight.

"Jeepers!" whispered Gus. "We sure done it that time, Joe."

Great-uncle's teeth were chattering like stones rattling in a dishpan. He never said a word.

Sim brought his lips up to my ear and said, "George! I told you."

"They *did* follow us," I said.

The chase died away. For a while we just lay there, waiting. There were two more shots, up toward town. They seemed to be more than a block away.

I raised up on one elbow. Everything seemed quiet. I turned to Sim.

"You can get up now," I said. "The danger's past."

"You sure, Old Timer?" Great-uncle Joe asked hoarsely.

"I'm sure," I said. "We're all alone here."

I was never more wrong. All of a sudden there was a rush of footsteps and a bull-like roar burst upon us. A flashlight was turned toward us; it was so bright I had to close my eyes against it.

"You're all under arrest!"

It was Mike Kurth.

"Git into that wagon and drive up to the jail," commanded Mike.

"It's me, Mike," I hollered.

"I know you. I know all you kids. I know some of them farmers out west of town, too. I don't trust 'em," hollered Mike in a voice that carried across the river. "Git into that wagon!"

"But you can't arrest us," I protested.

"I can arrest anybody breaking the law in my jurisdiction," shouted Mike. "I'm doin' it. You're all under arrest, every last one of you."

"But we ain't done nothin'," complained Great-uncle.

"Ain't done nothin'!" repeated Mike, amazed at such ignorance. "Disturbin' the peace! Shootin' off firearms in the village limits! Holdin' up the train! Aidin' a fugitive to escape! Ain't done nothin'! Ha! You call that nothin'?"

"I shot the gun," said Gus. "Arrest me, then, an' let the rest go."

"I'm arrestin' the lot," said Mike.

"Not this girl, Mike," I said. "She couldn't help what we did. She was just along with us."

Mike turned his flashlight directly upon Molly. Girls can always look as sweet and innocent as a lily with dew on it, and right then Molly looked just like that. It sort of shook Mike.

"Well . . . ," he said. "She don't look guilty."

"Mike," I begged, "take us, but drive this innocent girl up to my folks' place and tell Ma to take care of her."

Mike heaved a deep sigh as if to signify what a soul-struggle he was being put through. "Well, all right," he agreed reluctantly. "I'll do it. Ain't no room in the jail for her, anyway. Now move—git into that wagon!"

We climbed into the wagon, Mike after us. He stood there with his hand on the butt of his pistol, guarding us, and directing Great-uncle Joe to drive on up into Sac Prairie.

I could hardly believe it, it seemed so unreal, but we were on the way to jail!

17.

Under Arrest

THE jail in Sac Prairie was a square room with bars on the window—the single window that looked out on the street—and with a big iron cage occupying about half that room. There was hardly space for more than two cots and the four of us. The worst of it all was that the jail was only a block and a half from our place and only two blocks from Sim's house in the other direction. It was a funny feeling, but I felt I had never been so far from home.

Gus Elker was almost too stunned to speak. "Me," he said. "The Justice a the Peace—in jail! I don't know what we done, an' that's a fac'!"

"You poor dumb fool!" said Great-uncle bitterly. "I tol' you to leave that gun to home."

"This ain't legal," said Gus. "We can sue."

Great-uncle was not so sure. "Let's jest wait and see," he said.

"Where's Mike gone?" asked Gus.

"He took Molly up to our place," I said.

Sim just looked at me and shook his head slowly. "I should've gone fishing that day," he said. "I don't know why I listen to you, Steve. I got to get into the habit of doing the exact opposite every time you come up with some idea like this."

"As soon as Mike gets Molly up there, he'll be back," I said. "And don't you think even Mike can get away without making some kind of explanation to Ma. She'll pin him down, and he'll meet his match. Mike won't be alone when he comes back."

Mike wasn't alone. Grandfather Adams was with him. I guessed at once that he had intercepted Mike and fobbed Ma off.

I was never so glad to see him in my life as I was then. Even though he just stepped into the jail beside Mike, with a big cigar smoking in his fingers, and leaned up against the wall and shouted, "Great God in Heaven!" and laughed until the tears rolled down his cheeks.

"Grandpa," I hollered, "it's not funny."

"Oh, it is to me," he said. "It's funny all the way through. Here are my fellow Mill Creek Irregulars—in jail! And I can't bail you out, either—not until the judge sets the bail."

"I sent for him," said Mike.

"Not Elgy," I cried.

"He's the Justice here," said Mike. "Sure, Elgy. You want me to go to Baraboo and fetch Judge Hill down?"

I looked at Grandfather Adams, who stood there wiping his eyes and chuckling. "How's Molly?" I asked.

"A little shaken up, but all right," he said. "She'll recover. They've gone out to arrest Jake."

"What'd he do?" asked Gus.

Grandfather just smiled.

"How about George?" I asked.

"They winged him," said Mike as proudly as if he had done it himself.

"Who?" I wanted to know. "Who winged him?"

"Why, them Chicago detectives," said Mike.

"You mean you let Chicago detectives operate in your jurisdiction, Mike?" asked Sim slyly.

Mike's face underwent a transformation. "That's right," he said, as if a great truth had just dawned on him. "They never asked me, either. They jest told me. My jurisdiction! It's *my* job to arrest that feller George."

Grandfather Adams interposed. "Don't let the boys rile you, Mike. Those fellows got only one prisoner—not counting Jake, who's out of your jurisdiction. You got four."

Mike brightened immediately. "That's right! I done four times better'n they did."

The jail door opened and the Justice walked in. Mr. Elgy was something you could hardly believe was real. He looked like a shrunk-up undertaker, with dark bags under his eyes, and a face and head like a forever hungry rat. The way he conducted the Justice court was a crying shame or a shoulder-shaking joke, depending on which side of the law you were on. He was like a character out of *Alice in Wonderland*. You could just hear him hollering, "Sentence first—verdict afterwards!" He had been known to pronounce sentence without hearing the evidence, and on one occasion he had solemnly fined himself and presented the money to the village clerk.

"What's all this? What's all this?" he said, putting on black-rimmed spectacles and looking around him. "Four prisoners!" he exclaimed, and rubbed his hands together as if he were visibly adding up the fines he might impose. "What's the charge?"

"I got more'n one charge," said Mike.

"Well, well," murmured Mr. Elgy and smiled like a cat about to lap up a bowl of milk. He looked hard at us, and his face changed expression a little. He had recognized us. He clucked. "Steve Grendon! Now your grandfather won't like this at all."

"Which grandfather?" asked Grandfather Adams so suddenly that Mr. Elgy jumped.

"Both grandfathers," said Mr. Elgy. He looked again. "And Simoleon Jones! I always thought you were *good* boys."

"They were there, all right," said Mike. "I arrested 'em all. Shootin' off firearms in the village limits. That's the first charge. I got the gun."

"Hol' on!" hollered Gus. "That's my gun, and I done the shootin' with it. Not the boys."

Grandfather Adams began to laugh again. He just shook with laughter.

"You pleading guilty?" asked Mr. Elgy.

"No, I ain't," shouted Gus. "That feller ris up in Jake's coffin an' he had a gun in his hand an' I rolled over an' grabbed mine. It went off accidental."

"That's right," Great-uncle Joe and Sim and I said all together.

Grandfather Adams gave Mr. Elgy a fierce glance and said, "Looks as if that disposes of the charge."

Mr. Elgy sort of shook himself, smiled, and said, "Charge dismissed."

"Disturbin' the peace," said Mike promptly.

"Well, now," began Mr. Elgy, licking his lips. "We'll have to look that up in the statute book."

Grandfather Adams interrupted again. "I don't know, Mr. Elgy, as to how you can sustain that charge, either. If a man's gas tank blows up, you can't arrest him for disturbing the peace, can you?"

"Course not," said Mike. "That's a accident."

"Seems to me this is equally an accident," said Grandfather.

Mr. Elgy began to nod. "Fair's fair," he said. "We'll have to dismiss this charge, too."

I could see Grandfather Adams' eyes fairly dancing with merriment. He was certainly enjoying himself. For him it was better than any comedy at the movies. He always said people were more fun than anything else on earth.

"Well, they can't deny they opened that long-box," said Mike Kurth. "They helped George Riley to get away."

"The question is, did they know he was in the coffin?" asked Grandfather.

"If we known he was in her, we sure wouldn't a opened that box," said Gus fervently. "You think we're crazy?"

"That's a lead question," said Grandfather Adams, bursting into laughter again. "Don't insist on an answer."

"What were they doin' down there, anyway, if they didn't know George was in the coffin?" demanded Mike truculently.

"We were after that long-box," I said.

"What for?" asked Mike bluntly.

I told him. Sitting there on the jail bed telling it, I thought it was just about the silliest idea I ever heard.

When I came to the part about putting Molly into the long-box and shipping her down to Prairie du Chien, Grandfather Adams just broke down and howled. He had to lean against the wall to hold himself up. Mr. Elgy was grinning, too, but Mike just stood there staring at us as if he couldn't believe it. At that moment I could hardly believe it myself.

"We don't even know what George Riley did," said Sim hastily, as if to change the subject.

"He and some other fellers robbed a bank," said Mike. "They caught them other fellers and they got most of the money back some time ago. George is the last one."

"I be dog!" said Gus. "If we known that you couldn' a druv me to that coffin with a gun in my back."

"Just the same," said Mike doggedly, "they opened that long-box. George got out."

"But did he escape?" asked Grandfather.

"That's a fine point in law," said Mr. Elgy soberly.

"Well, you're the Justice," said Mike. "You ought to know the law."

"He ain't the on'y Justice," hollered Gus. "I'm Justice a the Peace, too."

"You tell him, Gus," said Great-uncle. "We can sue for false arrest."

"Hold on, now," said Mr. Elgy excitedly. "One thing at a time. We have to keep order in the court."

"This is the jail, not the court," said Great-uncle.

"Court is wherever the judge sits," said Mr. Elgy with a show of dignity.

"That's right," agreed Gus.

"And the first thing," Mr. Elgy went on, "is to settle this charge about aiding a fugitive to escape."

"How can we aid a fugitive if we don't even know he's there?" I demanded.

"And we don't even know he's a fugitive?" said Sim.

"The boys have a point there," said Grandfather, chuckling.

At that moment the outer door opened and Mr. Barton walked in. He stood there and took a look around. He saw me in the cage and grinned.

"I told you, boy, curiosity might get you into trouble," he said.

"Mr. Barton," I said, "did you get George?"

"We got him," he answered. "He's on the way to Chicago right now."

Mike Kurth came pushing up to him. "Say, Barton," he said fiercely, "how come you operate in my jurisdiction without letting me know?"

"We notified you, Mr. Kurth," said Barton mildly.

"You didn't get my permission," said Mike.

"We don't need it," said Barton. He took his billfold out of his pocket and opened it. "The whole United States is under our jurisdiction without license from local officers."

"Oh, you're the Secret Service," said Mike, immediately awed. "Why didn't you say so?"

"No need to. We were after a bank robber we suspected was coming into your town, and we got him."

"How come the Secret Service gets into this?" asked Mike.

"That bank the boys robbed was a Federal Reserve bank. We were called in, Mr. Kurth."

"And Jake?" I asked. "What about him?"

"We met him just driving into town," said Barton. "One of you men should drive his truck home. It's up here at the depot."

"I'll do it once I'm outa here," said Gus.

Barton looked at me and grinned again. "Did you get the girl?"

"She's up at our place," I said. "Mike was going to arrest her, too, but we talked him out of it."

Barton turned to Mike. He pointed at us behind bars. "What's all this for, Mr. Kurth?"

Mike told him.

Barton began to laugh. Mike got red. When Barton sobered up, he said, "Don't be silly, Mr. Kurth. These people didn't know anything about George being in that coffin. We didn't know ourselves. We had reason to suspect he was heading this way, because Jake's his only relative in this part of the country."

"That's a pretty long shot," said Grandfather.

"Oh, it wasn't so long," said Barton. "We intercepted a letter of Jake's to one of George's addresses. They were planning it, but George slipped away before we got to him."

"You sent George all alone with Mr. Morton?" I asked.

Barton grinned. "Boy, there were four of us. You saw only two of us, and that was no accident."

"What about Jake?" I asked.

"We'll put a charge of aiding and abetting against him," said Barton. "He doesn't count for much. He's mean and lazy, but outside of that . . ."

"Tryin' to force Molly to git married," put in Great-uncle. "Ain't that something?"

"She won't need to worry about her stepfather for a while," said Barton.

"Then she won't have to go away," I cried. "She'll be eighteen next week and come into her money. She'll be her own boss."

"She can stay with Lou and me," said Great-uncle.

Grandfather Adams looked at Mike. "Better unlock that cell, Mike," he said.

Mike was reluctant to do it, but he had no choice. Barton was laughing at him and Mr. Elgy had dismissed the charges and Grandfather was as firm as a rock, the way he looked at him. He came over and unlocked the cage.

"I got to do my duty," he said loudly, as if he were trying to convince himself.

"That's right, Mike," said Grandfather consolingly. "Better to lock the door before you find out than after. It might be too late then."

"That's what I say," said Mike, beaming. He smiled at us and said, "No hard feelings, boys."

We were glad to get out of that cell. We were glad to get out of the building.

"I got to git me my wagon and my team," said Great-uncle Joe.

"They're right around in back the jail," said Mike.

"Then I figger I'd better git Molly," said Great-uncle. "And take her back to my ol' woman."

"As for you boys," said Grandfather. "I think you'd better stay in town now you're here."

"But our stuff!" I protested.

"I'll drive you out first thing in the morning," said Grandfather, "and you can pick it up."

"Get mine, too," said Sim. "And thank your Aunt for me for all that good food and everything." He gave me a long, cold look and said, "Tomorrow I'm going fishing—and nobody's going to talk me out of it."

I didn't have the heart to remind him that his best fishing gear was out at the farm.

Mr. Elgy and Mr. Barton walked away together. Gus walked up the street with Grandfather and me to get Jake Riley's truck, so he could drive it home. Sim went east, and Great-uncle Joe came driving around with his wagon. Only Mike Kurth kept on standing there, watching the last tattered remnants of his dreams of glory vanish into the moonlit night.

It wasn't until I got within sight of the house that I thought of Mother. I stopped in my tracks. "Oh, gosh!" I said. "Ma! Does she know it?"

"How could she help knowing it?" asked Grandfather. "With Molly there."

"But Molly didn't actually see us in jail," I said.

"Well, that's so," admitted Grandfather. "But don't put your trust in miracles. There goes your Great-uncle. He'll let the cat out of the bag, depend on him."

The wagon stopped in front of the house and Great-uncle got out. The porch light went on, and Mother came to the door. We were close enough to hear everything he said.

"I come for Molly," he announced. "My, but it sure was a hard bed in that jail!"

Right there it was—almost the first thing he let out. I groaned.

"Jail!" hollered Mother. "Do you mean to say, Joe Stoll, that my son's in jail?"

"Oh, no. They let him out when Adams got there."

I ran up the porch and hollered, "All the charges were dismissed. We were helping to catch a bank robber."

"I'll attend to you later," said Mother.

Molly came up, on her way out of the house to join Great-uncle. "Thank you, Steve," she said.

Then she leaned over and *kissed* me. My cheek just burned.

Great-uncle and Molly went down the walk to the wagon.

"Seems to me it would've been smarter to let Molly go home in the truck," said Mother.

"Not with Gus Elker drivin'," Great-uncle shouted over his shoulder.

I went through the house to the kitchen. It was almost eleven o'clock. Father sat there reading *The Milwaukee Journal*. He looked around the edge of the paper and grinned.

Mother came flying into the kitchen. "To think of it!" she hollered. "A son of mine in jail! Oh, the shame of it! The shame! What will the neighbors think?"

"Ma, Mike just got too enthusiastic," I said. "We didn't do anything. We were just helping Molly."

"What will all the people think!" Mother hollered again.

"If you keep that up, they'll think he did something for sure," said Grandfather Adams, coming in.

"I know I shouldn't have let you go into the country," said Mother. "That Gus Elker! That Joe! And two kids like you. Well, I asked for it."

"You asked for it!" I hollered. "What happened to you? Nothing. It happened to us. We almost got shot. We saved Molly and because of us, they caught George."

"George who?" asked Mother.

"George Riley, the bank robber," I said.

Mother took a deep breath. "Stephen, I always did say you read too many detective stories. Tomorrow you start *Ivanhoe* or *Thelma* or *The Count of Monte Cristo*—something healthy." She shook her head. "My son—sitting in jail!"

She was all ready to start in again.

"Honest, Ma," I said, "he robbed a bank."

"I think all this has affected your mind," said Mother grimly.

I looked at Grandfather Adams. He raised his eyebrows and said, "Women are a race apart, Old Timer."

"When I think," began Mother, "of all the sacrifices Dad and I make for you kids . . ."

Father lowered his paper. His hand came smacking hard down to the table. "Enough!" he hollered. "You, Steve— go up to bed. Anything that has to be settled can be taken care of in the morning."

My own bed never looked so good to me.

18.

The Little Things

WHEN I got back from the farm next morning, I took Sim's stuff down. Most of it I left at the house, but the fishing poles and whatever else belonged there, I took to the harness shop.

Old Fred Jones looked at me over his spectacles where he sat sewing a hame strap. He grinned. "See who's here," he said. "I hear you been away."

"Sure," I said. "Far away."

"They keep that jail pretty clean up here?" he asked.

"Oh, so-so," I said. "I didn't see any fleas."

"Hot in jail?"

"Cool," I said. "Bricks and iron under all that shade—they keep cool."

Sim came rattling down from upstairs. His face was brick-red with annoyance. He had been sent up to clean John Ganzer's room again, and I could tell John had been needling him, too. By this time everybody in Sac Prairie had heard the whole story—and all the rest of the made-up stuff that people in Sac Prairie always tacked on to any story that went the rounds.

"It's about time you got here," said Sim. He almost tore the fishpoles from my hands.

"Oh, I guess the fish'll wait," I said. "They've been waiting ever since we went out to the farm."

"You don't need to remind me," said Sim.

"You figure the fish'll bite for a couple of desperate criminals?" asked old Fred.

"Pa has to pour oil," growled Sim. "He couldn't stop it no more'n he could stop breathing."

Fred chuckled. His shoulders shook. He went right on working with a dreamy expression on his face, as if he were thinking back to the time he was young like us. I didn't doubt but that he'd been in trouble once or twice, too.

"You going fishing?" I asked Sim.

"I said I was," said Sim. "I always do what I say— unless I get talked out of it."

"Oh, I guess you had fun enough," I said.

"He always has fun, but he hates to admit it," said Fred. "He leads a hard life."

Sim scowled. He examined the poles as if he feared I had handled them too roughly or carelessly.

I waited.

Old Fred said, "The jails down in the Philippines when I was in the War—now those were really dirty jails. You fellers had it lucky."

Sim clamped his mouth shut and refused to bite.

"They can hardly call you jailbirds," said Fred with a sly glance at Sim. "But they'll do it just the same. Jailbirds!" He rolled the word around on his tongue.

Sim was just about beside himself.

"Jailbirds," old Fred said to himself in a whisper.

Sim turned to me and said, "I got the worms dug. You coming along?"

"Sure," I said, "if you think it's safe for you."

"Come on, then," he said, and flung himself out the back door of the harness shop.

"Stay out of jail," Fred called after us.

"Pa just runs a thing right down into the ground," complained Sim.

I thought I'd better not say anything or Sim would remember to blame me for everything.

We went around the shop, through the narrow passage between the north wall and the little one-storey brick house beyond it, across the street, and up to the dead-end road that ran down beside the Electric Theatre. As always, we went over to look at the advance notices.

"Coming," read Sim. "John Barrymore in *Sherlock Holmes*. Soon."

"And another William S. Hart," I said. "I'd sooner have a mystery. Remember those Pearl Whites?"

Sim nodded and turned away. Down the slope, the river beckoned us. The Wisconsin was cobalt. A south wind blew, and little white wavelets washed up on the sandbar straight out from the shore. A few gulls flew low over the water near the old wing dam just across the river. On the east shore, the low hills looked hot. The grass there was drying for lack of rain, and cows dotted the hills, feeding on the false daisies and the St. John's wort and the harebells.

"School next week," I said.

"Don't spoil this morning, too," said Sim.

I knew what he meant by "too", all right.

We went around behind the retaining wall and found a place on the rocks there. We baited our hooks and threw in our lines. We settled back.

Oh, but it was good to be there! A few light fleeces floated over the hills on the other side of the river. Up at Karberg's bar some early swimmers were shouting and playing in the shallow water along the sand. The gulls were screaming now, and behind us rose all the noises of town—horses neighing, cars going by on Water Street, people talking, doors banging, kids hollering. Right here along the Wisconsin we were in another world. We were fenced in by the wall at our back, the willows crowding in out of the north, the river and the hills far up north and in front of us, the two bridges over the Wisconsin below us, even the railroad bridge far down.

Sim had a bite and pulled in a sunfish that was a good eating size. He smiled happily.

"I tell you, Steve," he said, after he had baited his hook once more, "if there's a heaven, I hope there's a place like this in it. They can just give me a pole and let me be. They can give you the harps—you can run the show."

"I don't want to run the show," I said.

"Hoh!"

A shadow fell across the water from the south. I looked up.

Grandfather Adams stood there. He was smoking a cigar and looking at us with a glint in his eyes.

"Why that glum look, boy?" he asked.

"Grandpa," I said, "things never seem to go the way I want them to."

"They never do—for anybody," he answered.

He came over and sat down next to us. He swept one hand out to embrace the river and the sky. "Here's a morning even a king couldn't order," he said. "Enjoy it."

"Grandpa, we are," I said.

"The cloud on your face would scare away the fish," he said.

"He hasn't even had a bite yet," said Sim.

I hadn't noticed it.

"All in all, things came out pretty well, didn't they?" asked Grandfather. "You saved Molly and the Secret Service men caught George."

"Our first case," I said, "and we had hold of it by the wrong end. That's what's the matter. What's saving Molly compared to catching a bank robber?"

Grandfather Adams smiled and clucked and shook his head. "Everything on this earth is relative," he said. "The smallest decent act is equal to the largest. That's in your Bible, too. Just between us, I'd sooner have saved Molly than caught a bank robber. I saw her kiss you."

"Grandpa!" I cried. My cheek burned all over again.

"Whoo!" hollered Sim, and began to laugh. "You got your reward, all right."

"Well, you got yours, too," I said hotly. "You *didn't* get kissed."

Grandfather laughed.

Sim pulled in a rock bass. "Look at this dandy!" he cried.

Grandfather said, "What you boys have to remember is

that you don't make the conditions for living. Life makes them. You just meet them—and the way you meet them shows what kind of men you'll be. As I look at it, the Mill Creek Irregulars did a pretty good job, and I'm not thinking of handing in my resignation as an honorary member yet."

"Well, Sim said it was George all along," I said.

"I didn't hear you say it wasn't," said Sim.

"No, that's right," I agreed.

"I always say," Grandfather Adams said thoughtfully, "the test of a man is what he does with what he has. You came pretty close to George without knowing why. You reasoned it out. After all, the men in the Secret Service knew all about his record. You didn't. They had the advantage of you, and you could hardly help that. All you had to start with was some neighborly suspicion and concern. It might have been somebody's overly active imagination. You did pretty well with it. If you always do as well, you'll do all right through the rest of your lives."

Grandfather Adams made me feel better.

"Look at that sun now," he went on. "Feel this air! Smell that water! What more would a man ask for on a morning like this?"

"Oh, it's fine," said Sim, "except that school starts next week."

"Well, boys, you take the bad with the good, and pretty soon you find out that what you thought was bad is pretty good, after all, and what you thought was good could have been better. You couldn't sit here and fish day after day. You go to school to apply yourselves to other ways of enjoying life and making the most of it. That's all you have to do—make the most of life."

"Grandpa, I do," I said.

"You work too hard at it," he said.

"That's what I always tell him," said Sim. "He has to learn how to go slow."

"There's an art to loafing successfully," agreed Grandfather.

"I can loaf as much as anybody," I said.

"That's an honest admission," said Grandfather. "Always be that honest with yourself."

"Well, we certainly made the most of the last two weeks," I said.

"We sure did," agreed Sim.

Grandfather Adams said, "If you always do as well, you'll be all right. Make the most of life, but don't do it at the expense of somebody else."

He got up, teetering perilously on the rock on which he stood.

"You've got a bite, boy," he said.

I grabbed my pole and pulled in a bluegill as big as Jake Riley's fat hand.

"Boy, what a whopper!" said Sim.

"And don't neglect the little things," said Grandfather Adams. "Like that."

"This?" I said, holding up the fish. "This is as big as anything right now."

"As big as the Mill Creek Irregulars?" asked Grandfather, laughing.

"As big as the Mill Creek Irregulars!" I said.

Grandfather Adams' laughter subsided into a broad

smile. He took a long puff on his cigar, and stepped back over the rocks toward the sloping ground beyond.

We settled down to fishing. I didn't tell Sim, but I was already beginning to think about what might come up next for the Mill Creek Irregulars.

A31